C SF

C

# THE MAN WITH BOGART'S FACE

## Andrew J. Fenady

**Thorndike Press • Chivers Press**
**Waterville, Maine USA  Bath, England**

This Large Print edition is published by Thorndike Press, USA and by Chivers Press, England.

Published in 2002 in the U.S. by arrangement with Arthur Pine Associates, Inc.

Published in 2002 in the U.K. by arrangement with the author.

U.S. Softcover  0-7862-4294-9   (Paperback Series)
U.K. Hardcover 0-7540-4983-3   (Chivers Large Print)

The text of this Large Print edition is unabridged.
Other aspects of the book may vary from the original edition.

Set in 16 pt. Plantin by Rick Gundberg.

Printed in the United States on permanent paper.

**British Library Cataloguing in Publication Data available**

**Library of Congress Cataloging-in-Publication Data**

Fenady, Andrew J.
  The man with Bogart's face : a novel / by Andrew J. Fenady.
   p. cm.
  ISBN 0-7862-4294-9 (lg. print : sc : alk. paper)
  1. Large type books. 2. Private investigators — California
— Los Angeles — Fiction. 3. Los Angeles (Calif.) — Fiction.
4. Lookalikes — Fiction. I. Title.
PS3556.E477 M36 2002
813'.54—dc21                                          2002020255

for Dashiell Hammett and
Raymond Chandler who put
it on paper
Humphrey Bogart and
Dick Powell who put
it on film
and
Gene Tierney from afar
and
Mary Frances from very
very near

# 1

*Dr. Inman had been a plastic surgeon for over twenty-two years. He had worked on thousands of patients, from famous movie stars to pathetic charity cases. And never did he have a patient with as bizarre a request as this.*

*Medically or ethically there was no reason not to comply. The patient had money, and after all, it was his face.*

*So Dr. Inman performed the operation. Now he was about to remove the man's bandages.*

*Yes — the operation was successful. The man looked exactly like Humphrey Bogart.*

After the bandages were removed the man with the Humphrey Bogart face slipped into a trench coat and a grey felt hat. The temperature in L.A. that July day was 92. There was no sign of rain.

He made a stop at the Los Angeles County Courthouse, where he had his name officially changed to Sam Marlow.

It's not all that hard to become a private eye. That was Sam's next move.

Then he bought two guns: a Luger and a

derringer. And plenty of lead.

Next he placed two ads in the Los Angeles *Times* classified section — and two ads in the *Valley Green Sheet.*

Sam had already rented a second-story office consisting of two rooms plus a toilet and kitchenette on the corner of Larchmont and Beverly. The office was over a doughnut shop. Across the hall there was a ladies' gymnasium.

He had also managed to buy a 1939 Plymouth coupe. He parked the vintage car in the vacant gas station on the north side of Beverly Boulevard and walked across the street, past the blind newsman on the corner and up the stairs.

Sam's office, complete with rolltop desk and ceiling fan, was just about ready for the Private Eye business. So was Sam. The sign painter was finishing the lettering on the frosted glass door:

SAM MARLOW
Private Investigator
"I Don't Sleep"

Some time later Sam was dozing in his swivel chair when the beautiful blond walked in and knocked on his desk.

Reflexively Sam pulled the Luger out of his

belt and pointed it between her breasts. At this — or almost any — distance it would've been hard to miss the titillating target. She was a honey blond, with flowing hair that fell in unstudied waves, big blue-green eyes, and luscious wet pink lips that looked like they had just eaten something sweet. She was in the medium height category but nothing else about her was medium. Her full-moon breasts swayed uninhibitedly over a small circle of waist; then she valentined into healthy hips tapering down long white well-turned legs to tiny feet. She wore a spaghetti-strapped polka-dot dress consisting of just about enough glossy synthetic material to make a pillow case.

The blond twittered and said, "I'm here about the ad you put in the paper."

Sam lowered his weapon and twitched his upper lip. "Which ad, Duchess?" Sam was a little sibilant when he talked. "I put in more than one."

"In response to being a secretary." Her voice was high-pitched and quavery — but sexy. Sam liked that.

"Oh, I thought maybe you were a client. I get two hundred a day plus expenses."

"That's terrific. How much do you pay?"

"For what?"

"For a secretary."

9

"*Times* or *Green Sheet*?"

"Come again?" asked the beautiful blond.

"Did you spot the ad in the *Times*, Duchess — or in the *Green Sheet*?"

"*Green Sheet* — it comes free."

"I thought so."

"Why?"

Sam's lip twitched again.

"*I'll* ask the questions."

"Could I just ask one?"

"OK, Duchess — let's say you got one coming."

"How much do you pay?"

"Oh, that again. One twenty-five a week — for the *Green Sheet*."

"That don't seem right."

"Why don't it?"

"Well — *you* get two hundred a day."

"Plus expenses," Sam added.

"How come the difference?"

"*I* take the chances."

The blond shrugged, and the movement sent out ripples all over her glossy polka-dot dress. "Well, my unemployment's run out. I'll take the job."

"I decide that." Sam's lip twitched again as he looked her up and down. "You're hired."

"Terrific."

"That's OK, Duchess."

"Could I ask you something else?"

"Ask."

"Aren't you hot in that trench coat?"

"Naw, I don't wear underwear."

"Neither do I," said the blond.

"I noticed that," said Sam.

"You know something?" Sam's beautiful blond new secretary added.

"What?"

"You remind me of somebody."

"Yeah, who?"

"I can't quite place it. But maybe it'll come to me while I sleep. Things come to me in bed." Duchess bent to pick up a paper clip from the floor. Her flowing honey-blond hair tumbled over her shoulders and her full-blown breasts heaved against the spaghetti straps that converged across her bosom. Sam held his breath as both breasts pushed and peeked out — but somehow the resilient polka-dot corral managed to contain the rest-less rounders.

Duchess put the paper clip on Sam's desk.

"See you in the A.M.," she said, and started to walk out of the office. What a walk. Sam's lips twitched.

"Good night, Duchess."

More than a month of good nights went by. Duchess looked like Marilyn Monroe and made as much sense as Gracie Allen.

Not that there was really anything to do around the office. But if there had been any messages, memos, or phone calls Duchess would have gotten them about as straight as her body. And Sam kept noticing that there was nothing straight about that. She was round and soft and sexy as lace pants — which she didn't wear.

The postman even made a point of bringing the "occupant" mail up to her personally instead of leaving it in the downstairs mail box. She reminded him of Annie Fanny.

It all really started that summer night. The overhead fan pushed the thick hot air around the room while Sam sat in the dark thinking about this and that, taking a couple of hits from the office bottle. The rent was past due and he was wondering where he'd move next. Maybe down by the porno picture houses. And he'd have to let Duchess go.

In over a month the phone had hardly rung. A couple of weeks ago there was a call from the Wilshire Chamber of Commerce and yesterday there was the obscene phone call. Duchess took down the message in shorthand as best she could. She made three or four tries at typing it out but finally gave up.

Then today Ripple Realty called saying the

rent was past due. That summed up Sam Marlow's career as a private eye.

Sam took another hit from the office bottle — then spotted the reflection in the window and heard the screech. The damned cat nearly scared the pants off him.

Standing there in the office holding the cat was the biggest woman he'd ever seen. Come to think of it, she was the biggest *anything* he'd ever seen.

"I'm Mother."

Whose? Sam thought to himself — King Kong's? But he decided to play it polite.

"OK. Want a hit from the office bottle?"

"I don't drink and neither should you." Mother had a voice like a hungry seal.

Sam poured himself another one — a double. The corner street light from outside illuminated the left half of Mother's huge face and body while the circling blades of the overhead fan sent shadows slashing across and down all seven feet of her.

"Is this business — or what?" Sam inquired.

"It ain't 'or what.' "

"I get two hundred a day plus expenses."

"That's heavy."

So are you, Sam thought to himself, playing it polite.

"Find Nicky for me."

"Who's Nicky — another cat?"

"Nicky's my boyfriend. He's disappeared. Here's a picture of us."

She pulled out a Polaroid and handed it over. Sam snapped on a desk lamp and took a hinge at the photo. Mother photographed like a giant suit of armor. But then that's what she looked like. Nicky had curly brown hair and a curly brown mustache. He photographed frightened and tired. Nicky came up to about Mother's elbow.

"He's disappeared," she repeated.

You probably swallowed him, Sam thought to himself, still playing it polite and remembering the rent and Duchess.

"Can you find him?" she asked.

"Maybe I can and maybe I can't."

"Will you take the job?" Mother's free hand went to her craggy forehead. The breeze from the fan had blown a shaft of her steely hair across her right eye. She tucked the wayward strand back into the iron web of her head.

Sam fired up a Lucky Strike. "Be careful how you move, Mother." He pointed to the overhead fan. "Those blades are just inches away from your hairdo."

"I said will you take the job?" Mother repeated.

"Maybe I will and maybe I won't."

"Your rent's past due."

Sam's lip twitched. "How do you know?"

"I own the building."

"How come I pay Ripple Realty?"

"They're rental agents. I own the building and the ladies' gymnasium across the hall. Find Nicky and we'll work something out."

"I can't use a bodybuilding course."

"Can you use some free rent? Find Nicky and I'll give you three months' free rent."

"Sounds OK."

"His name's on the back of the picture. He's Greek; I can't pronounce it."

"That's OK."

"Find him fast. Linda and I are lonesome."

"Who's Linda?"

The cat screeched again. "Oh," said Sam, stubbing out the Lucky in the ashtray, "a regular 'manage a twas.' "

"I don't stand for no dirty talk either. I know what that means."

Sam's lip twitched again.

"Say, what's wrong with your face?" she asked.

"Nothin'. Why do you ask?"

"How come you got a twitch?"

Sam pulled the Luger out of his trench coat pocket and placed it on the table. "This is a risky business, Mother. That's why I get two hundred a day — plus expenses."

"Not from me you don't. You get three months' —"

"That's OK. We got a deal. I'll have Duchess draw up a contract in the morning."

"Who's Duchess?"

"My secretary. Private."

"Yeah — I saw her going down the stairs," Mother barked. "There's not much about her that's private."

"The kid's swell."

"That's between you and her. Find Nicky."

"When did he take it on the Jesse O?"

"You said what?"

"Run out."

"He didn't run out. I think there's foul play."

"OK. When did you notice he was gone?"

"When I got back from Frisco. I was out of town on business. When I got back he was gone, but all his stuff is still there."

"Still where?"

"At our place. A little house on North Gower — 444."

"Cozy."

"Don't talk dirty. We're going to get married."

"That's between you and him." Sam pulled at the lobe of his left ear. "I'll drop around tomorrow and go through his things. Maybe

16

scare up a clue. Don't wash anything."

"What?"

"Shirts, shorts — stuff like that. Might be evidence."

"All right," said Mother. "But Nicky does all the washing anyhow."

"OK, Mother. We'll see if we can have him back before too much laundry piles up. Are you sure?"

"Sure about what?"

"That you won't have a hit from the office bottle?"

Mother turned around and walked out. As she opened the door she said, "Find Nicky."

Linda screeched.

Sam tucked the Luger back in his trench coat pocket and took another hit from the office bottle. The sweet sickening smell of simmering doughnuts was wafting up through the old-fashioned ventilation system. The phone rang. Sam took the Luger out of his trench coat pocket and placed it on the desk. Then, on the third ring, he picked up the receiver.

"Sam Marlow," he said.

"Oh, Mr. Marlow, thank heavens you're there . . ."

The voice on the other end was desperate but lovely. Sam figured her for a brunette.

"I need your help," the brunette said.

"I get two hundred a day plus expenses," Sam said.

Yeah, the private eye business was really picking up. In fact, in the last few minutes it had just doubled.

# 2

"Mr. Marlow, I'm desperate. I don't know where to turn."

"You just turned right, sister. What's the case?"

"Not over the phone," said the brunette.

"OK. Come on up to the office. My friends and I'll be waiting."

"Who are your friends?"

"Jim Beam and a cannon."

"No — please — can't you meet me?" implored the desperate lovely brunette.

"Sure — where's the meet?"

"At the Hollywood Bowl."

"Say again."

"Can you be at the Hollywood Bowl in half an hour?"

"OK. What's playing?"

"Nothing."

"Well then, why don't you save the tickets until there's something you want to see?"

"Please. I'll be in the center section of the Bowl, waiting. Make sure you're not followed."

"Listen, sister — how far can you follow a

wisp of smoke — how well can you see a . . . ?"
Sam realized he was talking into a dead
phone. The lovely desperate brunette had
hung up. Sam took a hit from the office bottle. Then he remembered something. She'd
forgotten to give her name. Well, that was
OK. How many brunettes would be sitting in
the exact middle of the Bowl when it was
closed?

Well, this is it, Sam thought to himself. Clients. Cases. Danger. Dough. Just like the old
days. The Saturday matinees. When there
were good guys and bad guys. When there
were Gables and Tracys — Garfields and
Powells (Dick and William) — yes, and Bogart — the one and only Bogart. The real arti-
cle. There was never anybody else like Bogart
— up to now.

Yeah, the old days. When there were causes
and flags and dames worth fighting for.

Sam checked the chamber of the Luger.
The slug was in there nice and snug, just waiting for instructions. He put the Luger in his
trench coat pocket. There was just one more
thing Sam had to do before he left the office.
He pulled open the deep drawer of the
rolltop, set the office bottle inside it, and lifted
something out. Sam took a look in the hand
mirror. His lip twitched.

Sam liked what he saw.

Sam locked the office, walked down the stairs, and started across the street to the closed gas station. He got into his car and started the engine. The Plymouth was a late '39 model — the kind with the gearshift up near the steering wheel instead of on the floor, like the early '39s.

You know, Sam thought to himself, Dana Andrews was swell in *Laura* — but just think if Bogart had played Lieutenant McPhearson. God almighty — just think of Bogart smoking his cigarette and looking up at the portrait of Laura. What a love scene. Man alive, thirty years ago Gene Tierney had to be the swellest, sweetest, sexiest twist in the war-torn world. Those eyes — a little Chinese. Hair — black as a raven's wing. The perfect curve of her patrician nose. Skin — white as snow on a twenty-thousand-foot peak. That lovely red, red mouth with teeth just a little too large, but white and sweet as sugar. The smile that knew so much but was still so secret. What dynamite she and Bogart would have been in that picture. Yeah, Bogart looking up at Laura. Thinking she was dead, but still in love with her. What a love scene. And neither one of them naked.

Sam shifted the Plymouth into gear. Then he thought of something. He flipped down

the sun visor. Yeah, it was there, all right —
the derringer, nice and snug in its custom holster. Sam slipped the derringer into his left
coat pocket and took off west on Beverly toward Vine Street.

Maybe the lovely desperate brunette would
turn out to look like Gene Tierney. Maybe.

He'd find out in fifteen minutes.

# 3

Sam steered the Plymouth north on Vine Street toward the Valley. The traffic was light as he drove past the Surplus Store on Santa Monica; it got a little heavy by Wallich's Music City as he crossed Sunset, and still heavier past the Brown Derby to Hollywood and Vine. Mostly summer tourists who would go back to Toledo and tell how they spotted Elizabeth Taylor going into the Pantages Theatre — or someone who looked just like her.

Sam grabbed a left on Franklin to Cahuenga, then right to the Hollywood Bowl cutoff. He drove past the combination Egyptian statue and fountain that hunkers over the entrance and parking lot. The lot was empty. Sam parked under a tree, flipped open the glove compartment, and took out a bag of unshelled peanuts.

He walked up the slanting pavement and looked toward the electric-blue sky that both absorbed and reflected the lights of the city. A few stars winked at Sam. Sam winked back, then cracked the shells of a couple of peanuts.

The Bowl was beautiful — like a high concrete cupped hand where 17,256 spectators could sit and watch and listen. But there was only one spectator sitting and watching and listening. The brunette. Right where she said she'd be. Sam walked up the extreme side aisle to her row, then started to walk across toward her. He was shelling and dropping peanuts as he walked. He even ate a few.

The brunette was sitting in Section H, Row 9, Seat 15. Only she was a redhead.

She didn't look anything like Gene Tierney. More like Elke Sommer — with burnished red hair. But lovely and desperate.

"Have a peanut," said Sam.

"Thank you," said the redhead.

"That's OK. I got plenty."

"No, I mean thank you for coming."

"That's my job." Sam sat in Seat 14. "I didn't get your handle."

"My what?"

"Your name." Sam spat out the skin of a peanut.

"Borsht."

"Once again."

"Borsht. B-O-R-S-H-T. Elsa Borsht."

"That's an unusual name."

"So is Sam Marlow."

"Check."

She looked at Sam. "Did anyone ever tell

24

you that you look like . . ."

"A detective — yeah. What's the caper, Miss Borsht?"

"Please call me Elsa."

"Thanks. Go ahead, Elsa."

"It's about my father. Lately he's been acting strange. Upset. Unstable."

"Sounds like he needs a doctor, not a detective."

"No. He's been getting phone calls and he's being followed by several men."

"Does he owe any bills?"

"No. Dad's a retired prop man —"

"Like in the movies?" Sam beamed.

"Yes. More than reasonably well off. Even our house is free and clear."

"Is there trouble with your mother . . . a divorce?"

"She's dead."

"Uh huh. Why did you pick this spot for the meet?"

"I work here in the office."

"Handy." Sam looked toward the huge arch of the stage. "Say, that'd be a swell spot for a Coca-Cola sign, wouldn't it?"

"I guess so." Elsa Borsht seemed a little confused.

"You know," Sam continued, "the acoustics here are among the finest in the world."

"Yes, I know." The redhead was still confused. "About my father —"

"What's his first name?"

"Horst."

"Horst Borsht?"

"That's right."

"These men who've been following him." Sam pulled at his ear lobe. "Have you ever seen them?"

"Yes. From a distance."

"I wonder if one of them looks anything like the fellow who's creeping along the aisle toward us?"

Elsa's head jerked around.

"He's been crawling on my peanut shells for the last two minutes." Sam pulled the Luger out of his trench coat pocket.

"Stand right up, buster, and make yourself known."

There was a slight wait, as if Buster were thinking it over. Then he stood up. Buster was holding a gun in his hand. Looked like a .38 to Sam.

"Well," said Sam, lifting his Luger, "I got one and you got one. Want to negotiate?"

"I think not." Buster smiled. "Look behind you."

"Not that old chestnut." Sam's lip twitched. "That one's older than Nero's Uncle."

"Meet Nero's Uncle," said another voice.

It could be heard very distinctly in the Hollywood Bowl.

Now the two gunmen converged, approaching Sam and Elsa.

"Such a lot of guns," said Sam.

"Put yours down on the seat in front of you. You wouldn't want the lady to get hurt," said Buster.

"I wouldn't want anybody to get hurt — on our side."

"Good. Put the gun down on the seat in front of you." Sam did. Buster was wearing a ski mask. So was Nero's Uncle. They were both average-sized men holding average-sized .38s.

"I intend to search you," said Buster.

"Go ahead."

"Miss Borsht. Step into the aisle above you."

"Do it," said Sam.

She did and showed a couple of shapely white thighs in the doing. Buster and Nero's Uncle came even closer to Sam. Buster laid his .38 down on a seat far away from Sam and took another step nearer the detective's right side. Sam's left hand was still in his trench coat pocket.

He fired the derringer through the pocket, hitting Nero's Uncle in the right arm. Nero's Uncle dropped the gun. In the same second

Sam backhanded Buster and sent him banging against the seats. As Sam went for his Luger both men ran in different directions and disappeared into the chocolate darkness. They could still be heard after they could no longer be seen — especially Buster, who backtrailed along the peanut shells.

Both of Elsa's birdlike hands were still covering her face as she stood shivering in the hot summer night.

"It's all right," said Sam, as he gently lowered her hands. "I'll take the case."

"Oh, thank you. Thank you," Elsa sighed, looking appreciatively into his face. Sam helped her over the seat; he couldn't help noticing the shapely white thighs again.

"There's only one condition," added Sam, "besides the money."

"Whatever you say."

"That's *it*," said Sam. "Whatever I say. I do the thinking for both of us."

"Yes."

She was standing close to him now. In fact, she was leaning against him. The full rounded front of her body still shivered a little — enough so Sam could feel it even through his trench coat. He touched her cheek with the tips of his fingers. She had to stand on her toes to reach him.

The kiss was soft enough. And moist

enough. And long enough — too long.

Sam pulled away and twitched. "I think we'd better go see your father, the prop man."

All she could say was, "Yes."

Sam took her by the hand and started to walk. "By the way, how did you happen to call me on the case?"

"I saw your ad in the paper. 'Private Investigator — I Don't Sleep.' "

"*Times* or *Green Sheet?*"

"*Times*," said the redhead.

"I thought so."

"Why?"

"Never mind. Damn, these shells are noisy. Oh, just a minute," said Sam. "You stay here."

He walked back and picked up the guns — including his Luger.

Sam drove the Plymouth toward the address she had given him in the Los Feliz area. He had put the two .38s under the seat, careful not to touch anything but the trigger guards.

"Say," Sam said, "did your dad ever work on any John Wayne pictures?"

"I'm not sure."

Sam rubbed his chin and thought, this kid's not as bright as she first seemed. How can she not be sure of something like that? But Sam

29

intended to ask Horst Borsht as soon as he got the chance.

"You know," Sam mused, "this area hasn't changed all that much since they shot *Double Indemnity*."

"Shot who?"

"*Double Indemnity*, right around this neighborhood. Paramount 1944. Edward G. Robinson, Barbara Stanwyck, and Fred Mac-Murray. Did you know Dick Powell was dying to get the MacMurray part? Wanted to change his image from a crooner to a tough guy. But MacMurray was under contract to Paramount. He was good, too."

"I think I saw it on television."

"Yeah, Stanwyck's ankle bracelet coming down the stairs. She wore a blond wig. Powell got his chance a little later."

"With Stanwyck?"

"No — Claire Trevor and Anne Shirley over at RKO. I remember . . ."

"The house."

"What house?"

"Our house. You just passed it."

"I know."

"Why?"

"In this business, Elsa, it's best not to park in front of the place you're going into."

"I see."

"I said I'd do the thinking for both of us."

A few more yards and Sam pulled the Plymouth over. Another car was parked across the street. There was a man inside it, smoking a cigarette.

As Sam and Elsa walked up the pavement to her house a car horn honked three times. Almost immediately two gunshots went off inside the house. Sam shoved Elsa to the ground, ran up the three steps, and kicked in the door.

One man was bleeding where he had fallen in an overstuffed leather chair, a gun still in his hand. The other man was still holding his gun pointed straight at Sam. There was more gunfire.

The slug tore a hole across the left sleeve of Sam's trench coat as he fired the Luger twice through his pocket toward the man. The first slug hit the man's heart. The second slug hit the first slug.

Overkill. But Sam didn't know it at the time — or care. The man dropped deader than a can of corned beef.

Sam went over to the man on the chair. It was Mr. Borsht. He'd never live out the minute.

Now Elsa was at the door. In his last second Borsht must've seen her as well as his whole life. He said something in German.

Then Horst Borsht died.

31

# 4

Sam never did get the chance to ask Borsht whether he had ever worked on a John Wayne picture. But Sam did ask Elsa what her father said just before he went over.

She wasn't sure, but she thought he'd said, "Ein Schlag" — translation, "A hit."

"OK," said Sam, "I'm going to call the gendarmes. We tell them everything the way it happened. You better go into another room — this isn't pretty — make some coffee."

"All right, Sam," she sobbed and started for the kitchen.

"Oh, and Elsa — you're aces. You got moxie. I take mine black with a dollop of sugar."

Sam made the phone call to Homicide. In short order the place was crowded with cops and other concerned parties, including newspaper reporters and photographers.

The officer in charge was Lt. Marion Bumbera. Second in command was Detective Sgt. Horace Hacksaw. They both listened to Elsa and Sam's story. Neither knew what to make of Sam. But the reporters and photographers did. They blazed away with questions and cameras.

There was a barrage of unimaginative queries about Sam's appearance. "Were you ever in the movies?" Sam just smiled. "Are you related to anyone who was ever in the movies?" Sam just smiled. "Are you a ghost?" Sam just smiled.

One reporter asked, "Weren't you scared when this gunsel pointed his rod at you?"

"Mine's bigger," Sam replied as he hefted his Luger.

Cameras went off again.

"That's all," said Bumbera. "Out! Everybody who's not in my department — *out!*"

Sam started toward the door.

"You, with the trench coat. You stay!"

"Sure, sweetheart."

"And don't call me sweetheart. The name's Lieutenant Bumbera. By the way, let me see your license."

Sam showed him.

A look of impatience flushed up Bumbera's face. "Not driver's license. Investigator's license."

Sam showed him.

"I'll be damned," Bumbera said. "Take a look at this." He handed the license to Hacksaw.

"I'll be damned," said Hacksaw.

Bumbera was not a big man but there was something imposing about him. Maybe it was his face. It looked as if some time or other it had been hit hard with an iron frying pan. Hacksaw wasn't quite as tall as a lamp post or as wide as a Frigidaire. His nose looked like a cherry Popsicle and his fists could've been a couple of cement cantaloupes. In the old days he would've been played by Nat Pendleton or Guinn "Big Boy" Williams.

Another cop came in carrying the .38s from the Plymouth that Sam had told them about. The guns and the stiffs were taken away for further study.

Bumbera instructed Sam to drop by headquarters tomorrow morning and not to shoot anybody else unless it was absolutely necessary.

Sam agreed on both counts. The party was over.

Sam told Elsa he'd see her tomorrow. He gave her a couple of seconals and put her to bed. He found a bottle of Horst's schnapps and took a couple of hits of Old Grand Dad — and fell asleep on the chair where Horst Borsht had died.

Sam woke up early. He checked on Elsa — she was still asleep. She had thrown off the sheet — there were those shapely thighs again. Sam covered them with the sheet and left.

He drove to his apartment on the 500 block of Larchmont, just a few blocks from his office. It was a three-story brick building built in 1930. Sam's apartment was on the second floor. He showered, shaved with his straight razor — it was only a two-nick shave — applied the styptic pencil, dumped a scoop of vanilla ice cream into half a cantaloupe, ate it, and went to headquarters.

Bumbera told him that both the stiffs were still dead. The gunsel was called Joe Kango and had a string of aliases long as a freight train. They were waiting for more dope on him. Bumbera asked Sam some of the same questions as last night. Was he sure he couldn't identify the parked car or the man in it?

"Nope — too dark. Too far away. Anyway, all these late-model cars look alike to me."

No more questions.

Sam made a couple of other stops, then headed for his office. He parked the Plymouth at the gas station and crossed the street to the doughnut shop.

The blind newsman on the corner told Sam that there was a real good picture of him on the front page of the morning paper and gave him a copy free of charge. There were four or five ladies from the gymnasium of assorted sizes and ages hanging around the hall to get a look at Sam. Mother poked her head out the door.

"Did you find Nicky yet?"

35

"Not yet, Mother."

"Well, what've you been doing? Find him."

"Yes, Mother." Sam opened the door to his outer office.

Duchess was on the job. The phone was ringing; she was trying to type with one hand and write something with the other.

"Oh, Sam," she twittered, "this place is a regular beehive this morning. I don't know what to do first."

"Don't do anything," said Sam as he lifted the receiver from the cradle and placed it on her desk.

She held up a newspaper. "Gee, that's a swell picture of you in the paper. You're famous."

There was Sam's picture with the caption, *"Mine's bigger, says Bogart look-alike — Private eye guns down killer."*

"Not bad." Sam's lip twitched.

"Say, I see you got a new coat," Duchess remarked.

"Yeah," said Sam, "the old one was full of bullet holes and powder burns."

"Oh, there's a lady here to see you. I shooed her into your office."

"Yeah, the redhead," said Sam. He opened the door and went into his office. He didn't hear Duchess say, "But she's not a redhead. She's a brunette."

The brunette was sitting in Sam's chair. She swiveled around, legs first, as he came in the door.

She didn't look exactly like Gene Tierney — but close. Close enough.

Eyes a little Chinese. Hair black as a raven's wing. Patrician nose. Skin white as snow on a twenty-thousand-foot peak. Red, red lips with teeth just a little too large. She stood up on long lovely legs.

"Mr. Marlow," she said, "I've come to you because I'm quite desperate."

Sam licked his lips and closed the door.

# 5

"I'd sure like to do something about that," said Sam, "but I'm sort of booked up right now."

"Yes, I read the papers. But this will only take a few hours. I'd be eternally grateful."

"Eternally, huh? That's a long, long time."

She smiled. Sam could hear the background music — "the face in the misty light — those eyes — how familiar they seem . . ."

And she was fuller-bosomed than Sam remembered in the picture. She spoke again — a cultured voice. Vassar, or maybe Bennington.

"I'm prepared to give you five hundred dollars."

"I'm prepared to take it. What's your name?"

"I suppose you'll have to know."

"Only if you tell me."

"Gena Anastas. My father is Alexander Anastas. You've heard of him?"

"The Commodore?! Yeah. He's one of those Greek shipping tycoons the world is full of lately. So you're Greek, huh?"

"Well, I was born in the United States."

Sam pulled out the Polaroid of Nicky and Mother.

"Ever see this fellow before? He's the one on the left."

"No, I haven't."

"Well," Sam shrugged, "it was another case anyhow. Tell me about your case."

"There are some photographs . . ."

"There always are."

"Please!"

"I shouldn't have said that, Laura — I mean Gena. Go ahead."

"It was at a party. There was this handsome athletic fellow . . . I can't remember much — or don't want to . . . he must've put something in my drink — I woke up in that horrible motel. They had taken pictures . . ."

"They?"

"Yes, there are others involved. Petey Cane of Cane's Club has possession of the pictures."

"You've seen them?"

"Yes — I can't believe it all happened."

"Neither can I. How much do they want — and when?"

"Ten thousand. Today."

"Yeah? What about tomorrow and next month?"

"They promised . . ."

"They always do. You have the ten grand on you?"

"Yes. I thought if you came along . . . it might scare them. I wouldn't want Father to find out."

"Sure, kid. I'll go along."

"Thank you," she said. Very gratefully.

Gena put her arms around Sam. Her fragrant face and hair pressed against the side of his cheek and throat. He let her stay pressed for quite a while. She was a *lot* fuller-bosomed than he remembered.

Sam told Duchess to call Elsa after lunch and tell her he'd be in touch later. And he asked Duchess to help Elsa with the funeral arrangements. Duchess didn't understand what the hell Sam was talking about.

Sam drove the Plymouth toward Santa Monica Boulevard, where Petey Cane's Club was located. Gena Anastas sat next to him. Her perfume did wonders for the musty mohair upholstery of the old '39 Plymouth. Sam looked at her. What a profile — lovely.

He flipped the visor down, lifted the derringer out of its custom holster, and slipped it into the left pocket of his new trench coat.

"You're not going to have to use that, are you?" She seemed very worried.

"Lieutenant Bumbera told me not to shoot

anybody unless it was absolutely necessary."

"Tell me about the case you're working on."

"Nothing to tell."

"You shot a man last night."

"Two."

"I'll bet you were protecting a beautiful girl."

"I was protecting myself."

"What were they after? The men you shot."

"Me."

"I can tell you can keep a confidence. That's admirable."

"It's my job."


It was still early and Cane's Club was still closed when they got there. Sam knocked on the dirty window of the front door and a torpedo with an Eastern accent opened it.

"Da lady's expected." He talked like he had a mouth full of baked beans. "*You're* not."

"It's a package deal," said Sam as he pushed his way through.

"OK, turkey," the torpedo sneered. "You can come as far as the next door."

"I'll think it over," said Sam. He and Gena walked into the joint. It smelled of stale beer and booze and hadn't been swept from the night before. Or the week before.

"Where's Petey Cane?"

The torpedo pointed. "Mr. Cane's in his private office. Da lady enters. You don't."

"I'll think it over," said Sam. He nodded for Gena to go in.

"But I thought . . ." She looked worried.

"Go in," said Sam.

She did. The torpedo closed the door behind her and stayed with Sam. Sam waited about half a minute, took a Lucky out of a fresh deck, and put the cigarette between his lips.

"Nice place Mr. Cane's got here."

"We like it."

"Topless?"

"And bottomless."

"Very classy. Say you got a light?"

The torpedo nodded, reached in his coat pocket, and never got his hand out. Sam's fist hit the front of the torpedo's face and the wall hit the back of the torpedo's head. He slid to the dirty floor bagging Zs.

"I thought it over," said Sam to the sleeping torpedo. He opened the door, flipping the unlit cigarette on to the dirty floor.

"Oh," said Sam to the people inside, "I thought this was the men's room."

The people inside besides Gena were Petey Cane and a young, athletic-looking fellow. Cane was the George Raft type — in his fifties — wore an expensive suit — Carroll & Company or Eric Ross — a custom-made shirt and a twenty-dollar raw silk summer tie. The young athletic fellow wore white slacks and a pale blue Dior shirt and bulging muscles.

"Where's Ralph?" Petey snorted.

"Thinking things over. How's the business transaction coming?"

"We're all through."

"That's right — you are. Did you get your ten Gs?"

Petey Cane nodded.

"That the artwork?" Sam pointed to the large envelope in Gena's trembling hands.

Gena nodded.

"Open it — take a look inside. Make sure."

Gena managed to open the envelope, pull the negatives and 8 × 10s halfway out, and quickly go through them without revealing the contents to the men in the room. She pushed the pictures all the way back into the envelope.

"Yes," she said, flushed with embarrassment.

"OK," said Sam, "give 'em to me." She did. Sam tore the envelope down the middle and put the two halves on Petey Cane's desk.

Then he pulled the Luger out of his trench coat.

"Now listen good, you rotten punk — and you too, jock. The deal's consummated —

signed and sealed. If you got any more of these — burn 'em. Because if any turn up or you ever bother this girl again I'll come back and blow holes through both of you the size of eggplants. And you, jock, guess where your hole'll be!"

Sam's hand was a little unsteady, and everybody in the room, including Sam, knew it.

"You're awful close to getting those holes right *now!*" Sam said.

Gena moved toward him. Sam threw a left hook flush on her lovely profile — but careful not to break her jaw. Down and out she went.

Sam switched the Luger to his left hand and sent his right fist crashing against the jock's jaw. Sam made sure he broke that one.

Then he turned toward Petey Cane, who shrank three sizes.

"You're a rotten punk and you're too old for me to slug. But I'm gonna do it anyhow."

He did.

It came down to the fact that Sam was the only one conscious in the room. He looked things over for a minute, then moved toward the ten crisp thousand-dollar bills and the torn envelope on Petey Cane's desk.

It couldn't've been more than three or four minutes later that Sam was helping the still dazed Gena out the alley door of Petey Cane's Club.

"Why — why did you hit me?" she asked.

"I'll explain later. The money's in your purse. You won't be bothered again."

That's when a man stepped out of a doorway and hit Sam behind the ear with a sap. Expertly!

# 6

In the autumn of radio's dramatic life Dick Powell did a detective series called *Richard Diamond*. Two or three times an episode Diamond would get sapped behind the ear and land on cloud nine. Other detectives in other versions would dive into a black pit — with no bottom. It was always a relatively painless experience that allowed for a little narrative recapitulation of the plot — or sometimes a commercial break. The detective always woke up, rubbed the lump behind his ear, and went about the business of the next act with little or no residual effect. That's not the way it happens when you get sapped — and Sam could tell the world.

It's pain, brothers and sisters, pain. With a capital P — that rhymes with T — and stands for misery — and coming to is even worse. It's worse than the worst hangover. It's a hundred rattlesnakes loose in your skull. It's ice picks sticking into the back of your eyeballs. It's a hot poker going in one ear and out the other — that's what it is, sisters and brothers. But slowly you do come out of it — and so did Sam — slowly.

He was first dimly aware of what seemed to be the ceiling of the saloon of a sailing ship or yacht. A lantern swayed from the ceiling and the room billowed. The sound of a roaring sea battered the vessel. Or so it seemed in Sam's dented brain.

Then, still slowly, things settled. The sound subsided. The sea calmed and the room leveled off.

Sam could finally discern an out-of-focus man — a tabernacle of a man, gray hair, strong wind-rubbed face, prominent nose with dark steel-rimmed glasses. The man was wearing a double-breasted blue blazer with glittering gold buttons.

"Is he coming out of it?" Sam heard him say.

"Yes." It was Gena's voice. She was kneeling by the leather couch next to Sam, applying cold towels to the side of his head. Somehow, the glitter made Sam's head ache even more.

"You're a damned fool, George," the man said to George — whoever and wherever George was. "You almost killed him."

"That's a fact," Sam agreed to himself.

"I'm sorry, Commodore." It must've been George who said it but George didn't really sound sorry to Sam. Not that it made much difference to his head.

Sam started to rise, wobbled, then settled for sitting while his palm tried to soothe the walnut behind his ear. He took a good look around the room and decided they weren't really on a ship. The room was just designed and furnished like a boat — but bigger, much bigger.

Then he took a good look at the people. There was Gena like an angel. And the tabernacle man — that had to be Commodore Alexander Anastas. Over to one side stood a beautiful olive-complexioned woman in her early forties who looked like Dolores Del Rio and was built along the lines of Patricia Medina.

Over to the other side — that just had to be George. He was built out of steel and catgut and wore a dark pencil-lined suit — probably size 44 regular. It was a little tight around the chest.

"I've been on boats before," said Sam, "but never piped aboard like this."

"Sam, are you all right?" Gena asked. It was a dumb question but she meant well.

"Peachy," said Sam.

The Commodore was a take-charge guy. He took charge. "I am Alexander Anastas. I rarely apologize, but I apologize to you, sir."

"That fixes everything," said Sam. "Except my head."

"George made an error in judgment. George is my man."

"Your man with a sap?" Sam started to rise. Negative. "Whoops, not yet. I think I'll just sit here for a while."

"This is my wife, Teresa," the Commodore motioned toward Dolores Del Rio-Patricia Medina. She smiled.

"Charmed," said Sam.

The Commodore started to motion toward George.

"I already ran into *him*," said Sam.

"George was under the impression that he was assisting Gena."

"So was I."

"Yes. Would you care to tell me why she came to you?"

"No."

There was a slight pause while the Commodore mulled over the monosyllable.

"That is your privilege, sir."

"In that case, I'll tell you. It *is* OK to tell him, isn't it, Gena?"

That worried look came across Gena's face again.

"She asked me to find an old school chum of hers. Vassar, was it? or Bennington?"

"Bennington." The worried look subsided.

"The chum ran away from home, had a habit, a big one — H. I got a tip that the chum was working as a topless dancer at Cane's Club. She wasn't. That's it."

"I thank you, sir." The Commodore seemed relieved.

"What for? I haven't found her yet."

This time Sam managed to get on his feet. He walked over to what looked like a row of display cases. They were filled with all kinds of doo-dads. Daggers, jewels, gold watches, ships' compasses, books, even bottles.

"I have a passion for collecting," the Commodore said.

"Yeah. I've got a passion for passion."

Sam noticed that the windows of the room were protected by steel bars.

"Most of these items are priceless," the Commodore went on. "Isabella's diamond ring, Napoleon's watch . . ."

"And my father's mustache," said Sam.

"Unfortunately, I won't be able to see these artifacts — or anything — much longer. I am going blind, sir. Not all my wealth, not anything — can prevent it. No power on earth or in heaven."

"That's too bad, Commodore."

"I sailed ships where nobody else would go. Harbors that were too shallow — reefs that were too dangerous — hauled cargo that no other man would carry. I built an empire, sir, and I'll live to see it fade into shadows and nothingness, soon — too soon."

"Yeah, well, enjoy it while you can, Commodore. Think I'll run along. I haven't built my empire yet."

"I am in your debt, sir. Please feel free to call on me if I can ever be of service."

"I'll do that. And you can start by telling me how I get off the Queen Mary."

"I'll show you the way," said Gena.

"Thanks."

They started toward the door. As he went by the Commodore's wife Sam nodded and said, "Mrs. Anastas, it's been nice talking to you."

She smiled. A handsome smile, but a little frightened. Like she was waiting for something to happen. Maybe for something permanent to happen to the Commodore, Sam thought.

"Oh, one more thing," Sam said. He picked up a small but heavy stool and smashed it across the back of George's head. "I don't sap so good on Tuesdays."

George had already hit the deck.

Sam's Plymouth was parked in the Anastases' driveway. So were a couple of Rolls Royces, a Mercedes limousine, a

Ferrari, and some other rolling stock, worth a total of at least a hundred fifty grand.

Sam's Plymouth looked a little out of place there in Holmby Hills. How the Plymouth had gotten there he didn't know — or ask — or care. His head felt a lot better since he'd caved in George's.

He got in on the driver's side of the Plymouth. Gena got in on the other side.

"Look, Angel, I got to get back to my beat."

She placed a thousand-dollar bill on the dashboard.

"The fee was five yards," he said.

"You did more than was expected."

"I did my job."

"Then consider the rest a retainer."

"I'm retained. But only if you promise to stay out of motels."

"I promise." She leaned across and kissed him. There was that background music again. All the other kisses in the world were just handshakes compared to this. She put her heart and soul and everything else she had into it. So did Sam. He knew it was only a prelude to what had to come later — yeah, later.

Sam broke away. "I got to get back to my beat."

"Can I come see you some time?"

"You don't even need an appointment. Just knock three times."

"I will. That was a beautiful lie you told about my chum."

"You've got a beautiful chum. Bon Sower."

She got out and Sam started to drive away after he put the G in his pocket. He looked back and saw her wave. His lip twitched. In fact, he twitched all over.

# 7

It took Sam about twenty minutes to drive from Holmby Hills to Larchmont and Beverly. He stopped at the bank across the street and made a deposit in his depleted account.

The office was still a beehive, and the Queen Bee still didn't know what to do first. She was trying a little bit of everything.

"Hello, Duchess."

"Oh, Sam, there've been a trillion calls."

"Did Elsa call?"

"Uh huh. I told her you'd call back. Oh, and an underwear company wants to know if you'd be interested in endorsing their stuff."

"I don't wear underwear."

"I told them that."

"What'd they say?"

"They wanted to know how I knew."

"What'd you say?"

"I don't remember."

"Maybe it'll come to you."

"Maybe . . . but I don't think so."

"Neither do I."

Sam started for his office. "Get Elsa on the phone."

"Who?"

"Never mind, I'll get her."

Sam did. Elsa seemed reasonably well.

"I think you better get out of that house," Sam said. "Look, Duchess has a spare sofa. She can sleep on it and you take the bed."

"No, Sam, really. I'd rather stay here."

"OK then. I'll come by with a couple of steaks later."

"Sounds good."

"They'll taste good, too."

Sam put down the phone. He was taking a hit from the office bottle when Duchess came in. Either her skirts were getting shorter or her legs were getting longer.

"Sam, there's someone here to see you."

"Who?"

"I think he said his name was Mr. Gazelle — is that important?"

"Is what important?"

"His name."

"I don't know."

"Neither do I." Duchess shrugged and sashayed toward the door. "I'll shoo him in."

"Do that."

She did.

"Mr. Gazelle?" Sam said.

"Mr. Zebra," said Mr. Zebra.

"Oh, sorry." Sam looked at Duchess — she shrugged and sashayed toward the door again. "Sit down, Mr. Zebra. But I don't think I can help you — I'm sort of booked up right now."

"Of course, but just a few minutes of your time."

"OK."

"Mr. Marlow, have you ever heard of 'the Eyes of Alexander'?"

"No."

"Have you ever heard of twenty-five thousand dollars?"

"Yes. What's one got to do with the other?"

"I am prepared to pay you twenty-five thousand dollars if you deliver me Alexander's Eyes."

Sam gave Mr. Zebra the double O. The fellow wore expensive clothes, which seemed a little too large for him. He was on the short side — maybe five feet eight. Had a little too much slickum on his hair. Face a little too pudgy and hands to match. He spoke slowly with a slight continental accent. Mr. Zebra smelled of too much perfume — lavender.

"Alexander who?" Sam inquired.

"Why, the Great, of course."

"Of course."

"Well?" Mr. Zebra arched both eyebrows expectantly.

"Well, what?"

"Is it acceptable?"

"It might be. Say, this Alexander's been dead for quite some time, hasn't he?"

"Of course. Over twenty-three hundred years."

"Well, what shape do you expect his eyes to be in?"

"Not his real eyes, of course."

"Of course." Sam took a hit from the office bottle.

"The eyes of the statue," Mr. Zebra said.

"Oh, *those* eyes."

"Of course."

"You know," said Sam, "if you say 'of course' enough times, it sounds silly."

"Of course."

"That's what I mean . . . oh, and these Eyes of Alexander — they're made out of whatchamacallit — again?"

"Sapphires, of course."

"Of course."

"Mr. Marlow, I get the distinct impression that you know much more than you reveal."

"That's the impression you're supposed to get."

"Of course. Here is my card. I have retained an answering service. Please call and leave word when you are ready to complete the transaction. The twenty-five thousand will be in cash, of course."

"Of course."

"As you Americans say, the sooner the better."

"That's what we Americans say all right."

"I thank you and bid you good day."

"Same to you."

Mr. Zebra stopped at the door and looked back at Sam, who was putting a Lucky between his lips.

"I expect the utmost discretion in this matter, of course."

"Of course."

As Mr. Zebra went out the door he said, "Mr. Marlow, you have a quaint secretary."

Sam spat out the unlit Lucky and took a hit from the office bottle. He could still smell the lavender, mixed with simmering doughnuts.

# 8

Sam called Bumbera, but Bumbera was out. Hacksaw was in — so Sam asked him. "Did you boys get a make on any prints from the guns?"

"No clear prints on either piece," said Hacksaw.

"Well, in that case," Sam asked, "what do you think of the international situation?"

"I'm not paid to think . . ."

"Right."

". . . about the international situation."

Sam figured there wasn't much future in this conversation. Hacksaw must have agreed — he'd hung up.

Sam told Duchess she could go home early. She said she wasn't going home. Sam said she could go wherever she was going early.

"Thanks," she twittered, "I'm going to the beauty shoppee."

"You've got enough already."

"Enough what?"

"Beauty."

"I'm going to get my legs waxed."

"Both of 'em?"

"Huh?"

"Never mind. Good night, Duchess."

Sam went out the door. He had a hand on the rail and a foot on the stairway when Mother poked her head out of her door.

"Find Nicky yet?"

"No. But I've got a clue."

"Screw your clue. I want Nicky!"

It sounded like Mother was getting desperate.

Feeling flush from Gena's G, Sam decided to splurge. He walked down Larchmont to Jurgensen's and bought two steaks. That killed the better part of ten bucks. Then he picked up a couple of artichokes and cucumbers and something special to drink — a six-pack of Michelob — the tab came to $13.33.

Sam parked the Plymouth a few doors past Elsa's house, tucked the groceries under his left arm, and started to walk down the street. A black car, driven by Lieutenant Bumbera, pulled up.

"Hello, Bumbera. I'd ask you to stay for dinner, but . . ."

"You movin' in here, Marlow?"

"That's none of your beeswax."

"You're right. Shoot anybody today?"

"Not yet, but it's early. Got any suggestions?"

"Be careful that gun doesn't go off in your pants."

"I wear a cup. Anything else?"

"Not today."

"Sleep good, Lieutenant."

"Yeah. By the way . . ."

"I figured there'd be a 'by the way.' "

"I did a little digging into your past."

"Yeah? Let me know if you can do any digging into my future."

"How's the wound coming along?"

"What wound?"

"You know what I'm talking about."

"Do I?"

"Want to know something else? Screwy as it sounds, I kinda like you."

"Yeah, well, before this turns into something disgusting I'd better get going."

"So long, shamus."

"So long, sweetheart."


Sam fixed up the steaks and artichokes. Elsa sliced the cucumbers and soaked them in oil and vinegar.

The dinner was good; the conversation was sparse. Sam drank three beers. Elsa drank one. They were running out of things to say when Sam asked if anything unusual had happened today. Anybody call? Or did she spot anybody hanging around?

"No, nothing and nobody. Oh, wait a minute. I nearly forgot. Something strange did happen. It doesn't make much sense. I'll get it for you."

"What?"

"The letter. It came in the mail today."

"To you?"

"No. To Father."

"Who from?"

"That's the strange part. It's *from* him *to* him and it doesn't make any sense. It's some kind of a poem. Father never wrote poetry in his life."

Sam grabbed another Michelob while she got the letter. It was still in the opened envelope, postmarked the day before and addressed by the same hand that had written the letter. Elsa was sure it was her father's handwriting.

> Under the tramp of marching feet
> Under the beat of daring drum
> Follow the three beneath the post.
> Age will show the way to go
> To a stone, a stone, high or low.

Sam read it to himself — then read it aloud. "This is tougher than the Musgrave Ritual," he said.

"What's the Musgrave Ritual?"

"A Sherlock Holmes story. It was made into a Universal-International Picture, 1943, with Basil Rathbone and Nigel Bruce. They called it *Sherlock Holmes Faces Death*."

"I think I saw it on television," Elsa said.

"Yeah, they run it all the time. Hillary Brooke and Milburn Stone were in it — but what was your father trying to say?"

"I have no idea."

"Now, Elsa, I know you went over all this with the cops and me last night — but try to think. Did your dad have any enemies? Where he used to work at the studios, maybe? Did he gamble? Could he've been involved in narcotics? Anything like that?"

"No, no, no. He was a quiet man. A private, very private sort of person. He still felt this was a foreign land."

"When did he come to the U.S.A.?"

"A few years after the war."

"WW Two?"

"Yes."

"Was he in the Army?"

"Yes."

"The Blitzkrieg Boys?"

"What?"

"Hitler's heroes."

Elsa nodded.

"You mind if I take this along?"

"Of course not."

"And don't say anything to anybody about this. It'll be our little secret." Sam put the letter back into the envelope and stuck it in his inside pocket.

"It's still early. You want to go out and see a movie?"

"No thanks, Sam. I think I'll get to bed. I'm going to go in to work tomorrow."

"What kind of a boss have you got?"

"Oh, no. They told me to take as much time as I want, but there are a few things I need to take care of. No sense in sitting around here all day."

"OK, Angel. I'll run along."

He got up and started to leave.

"Sam." She came over and put her arms around him. The kiss wasn't like Gena's, but it wasn't exactly a handshake either. "You make a terrific steak."

"Yeah," he said, "there's nothing wrong with your cucumbers, either."

# 9

Since it was still early Sam decided he might as well go back to the office. It was more conducive to deductive reasoning than his apartment, and he had plenty of deductive reasoning to do on that letter — or poem or anagram or whatever the hell Horst Borsht had meant.

More than two hours later Sam was still reasoning deductively — without results.

> Under the tramp of marching feet
> Under the beat of daring drum
> Follow the three beneath the post.
> Age will show the way to go
> To a stone, a stone, high or low.

"What the hell could that Dutchman have meant?" Sam said out loud. He'd tried everything. The first letter of each word. First letter of each line. Every other word. Nothing worked. Well, he'd give it another half an hour, then go home.

Sam was getting stiff from hunching over the letter. He swirled around, stood up, and stretched. Then he did a couple of squats and walked to one of the windows facing Larchmont. The windows had wooden shutters that folded in sections. Sam pulled the little knob on one of the sections and took a look up and down the boulevard.

This was one street that really rolled up the pavement early. By six all the shops were closed — markets, antique stores, beauty shops, the drugstore, all the banks, Jerry's Barber Shop, Chevalier's Book Store — even the two liquor stores. The only thing open on the block was the doughnut shop downstairs, where Bill, the manager, was simmering a fresh batch of sinkers.

The Larchmont shopping center was one of the few genuine villagelike communities left in L.A. — patronized by old rich and new rich, mostly women and practically all Republicans who lived in the Hancock Park and Windsor Square areas. Their husbands were mostly lawyers, doctors, insurance men, and stockbrokers. But that wasn't any stockbroker standing in the dark doorway across the street, looking up at Sam's window.

It was impossible to see the man's face in the darkness, and from this distance it was even tough to tell his size.

Sam gave the man a wave. The man didn't wave back. He walked out of the doorway as if he had just thought of something — hurried north and then right on Beverly.

Sam turned away from the window. He thought he'd heard a noise from somewhere in the office. There was nothing there.

He sat on the edge of the rolltop and re-capped the events since Mother's visit. The phone call from Elsa. The meet at the Bowl. Gunplay with Buster and Nero's Uncle. More gunplay at Horst Borsht's. Introduction to Bumbera and Hacksaw. New coat. His picture in the paper. Beautiful darling Gena and her pictures. Petey Cane and the jock. Time out for sapping. Commodore and company. And George, the family retainer. The kiss that could launch a thousand missiles. Mr. Zebra, smelling of lavender and offering twenty-five grand for a couple of mislaid sapphires. Duchess and her waxed legs. Dinner with Elsa. The letter from a dead Dutchman. A shadow across the street. Well, bright boy, Sam thought to himself, everything's up to date in Kansas City — all you have to do is figure out —

That's when he heard it again. Some kind of noise — maybe rats in the walls or the attic — maybe two-legged rats, Sam thought.

He checked the Luger. It was ready. So was Sam. He put the letter in his inside pocket and the Luger in his coat. There it was again

— louder, coming from above. Then that was the place to look.

He went out into the hall. Empty. Quiet. Dark. Sam walked to the rear of the hall and went up the stairway that led to the roof. This time he took the Luger out of his pocket. Why buy a new coat every day?

The panel that opened into the attic was about halfway up the stairs. Silently Sam pushed it open. It was just big enough for a man to get through. Sam looked in — about twenty feet into the darkness there was light coming from around a corner toward the front of the building where Sam's office was. He eased through the opening and carefully made his way toward the light.

He heard a sound from around the corner. Sam stopped, pointed the Luger at the corner, and waited. If anybody unfriendly came around that corner he'd buy one right in the belly.

Nobody came. Sam waited another minute — then another. OK, if Mr. Unfriendly wasn't coming to Sam, Sam would do the coming. Probably somebody spying on his office through the ventilation system — maybe one of the ski masks — Buster or Nero's Uncle — or both.

Sam eased ahead. He made the corner, stepped around with his Luger pointed, and said, "Evening, friend."

"*Jesus Christ!!!*" came the reply.

If Sam had shot he wouldn't've hit him in the belly. More like the Adam's apple.

"Well, well," said Sam, "if it isn't little lost Nicky."

"Will you, for Christ's sake, Mister, put gun down," said Nicky. He had a distinctly Greek accent.

"Sure, pal, glad to."

"Thanks, sport."

"So this is where you've been hibernating."

"What does that hiber— hiber— whatever you said — mean?"

"Resting."

"Yeah."

"Aren't you lonesome up here?"

"Not yet."

"You know who I am?"

"Yeah, I seen you when you move in — and few times after. Always I mean to stop in — pay visit."

"Well, it's never too late. Come on down and I'll buy you a drink."

"No. I stay here for while yet."

"How long?"

"Till I ready."

"For what?"

"For her."

"Well, she's ready for you right now."

"I know. Say, sport, don't I see you some time on television in old movies?"

"No. That's somebody else."

"He sure look like you."

"No. I look like him. How long you been up here?"

"Since day before she come back."

"What do you eat?"

"At night sometime I go to Ranch Market — open all night. Bring *fayee* — food."

Sam glanced toward Nicky's larder, which consisted of an old bench. On top of it were stacked many cans of oysters — bottles of vitamin E and gin — olives — carrots — figs — and various other potent nutrients, along with several issues of *Playboy* and *Penthouse* magazines.

"How long do you think it'll be before you're ready?"

"Few more days, maybe."

"You know she hired me to find you — she's worried."

"So I. Please no tell her. Not yet — few more days. I eat lot oysters."

"I don't know whether that'll do it, pal."

"I feel stronger — before she go — I how you say — drained. Exhaust. She big woman."

"I noticed."

"I love. But she love too much. I need how

70

you say hiber— hiber."

"Hibernate."

"You betcha. No tell yet — you understand — how you say — man to man."

"Didn't you rest up while she was gone?"

"After she gone week — she call — 'Fly up, Nicky,' she say — I do — two weeks San Frisco — exhaust. I fly back — when I hear she come — I hiber— hiber—"

"Hibernate."

"You betcha."

"Why, the little darlin' — she didn't tell me you were up in Frisco."

"Exhaust — you no tell yet."

"OK — I'll give you a couple more days. But *I* take you in. You're three months' rent to me."

"Sure. Sure."

"You want me to bring you anything to-morrow?"

"No. I be fine."

"OK. Say, how *do* you pronounce your last name?"

"Kalamavrakinopoulos."

"Yeah, well — so long, Nicky."

# 10

Half an hour later Sam was still in his office trying different combinations of decoding expertise. But Horst Borsht's puzzle was still a puzzle. Sam rubbed his eyes and took a hit from the office bottle. There was a knock on the door. Then another. Then another.

Holy Toledo! Could it be?

It was.

She was wearing a silky white summer dress that made her look even more like Gene Tierney. And the perfume wasn't lavender. Joy by Patou — a hundred dollars an ounce and worth it — at least on Gena.

"You said I didn't need an appointment."

"Angel, you don't need anything."

"It says on the door you don't sleep."

"It's just a slogan."

"But you do work late."

"Yeah."

"Why?"

"In hopes that somebody as beautiful as you'll knock on the door. Anybody ever tell you that you look like Gene Tierney?"

"A few times."

"You do. You're too young to remember her in *Sundown*. Bruce Cabot, George Sanders, Joseph Calleia . . . and at the end Cedric Hardwicke had a scene in a bombed-out cathedral. I don't think he was a 'Sir' yet. There was a shot when you — I mean, when she — walked across the desert wearing what there was of a sort of a silky costume — she had a walk that vibrated right off the screen — nothing more beautiful ever walked on a desert — or any place else — except you."

"Why, Sam, that's very nice. And it's the most I've ever heard you say."

"Me too. You never told me how you happened to come here."

"You said I didn't need an app—"

"No. I mean the *first* time."

"I saw your picture in the morning paper and read the story of what you did. I needed help. I think I came to the right place."

"So do I."

"I'm *glad* I came."

"So am I."

"Want to buy me a drink some place?"

"Any place."

"You never told me what you were working on."

Sam pointed toward the rolltop.

"A puzzle."

"Crossword?" She smiled.

"No. It's a letter from a dead man — say, that's not a bad title."

"The man you killed?"

"No. From the man who was killed by the man I killed."

"Mr. Borsht."

"Yeah, Horst Borsht. And the letter is as screwy as his name. About that drink —"

"Ready when you are."

Sam put the letter in his inside pocket and guided Gena toward the door. The way she walked sent vibrations right through Sam. He stopped. She knew why. She put her arms around him. There went the music and the missiles again. It seemed like the top of Sam's head would go too. This time *she* pulled away.

"About that drink."

"The drink can wait."

"Can't you, Sam?"

"I don't know. How long?"

"Not long."

They started toward the door.

"You know, you shouldn't be out on the streets alone."

"I'm not alone."

"That's right. Not anymore."

# 11

There was a black-and-white police car parked downstairs in front of the doughnut shop — and a team of black and white cops inside getting coffee-and. Bill waved to Sam, who waved back. But Bill and the cops weren't looking at Sam. Sam knew it. So did Gena. She was used to people looking at her and she could handle it.

They walked across the street to the closed gas station. A white Ferrari was parked next to Sam's Plymouth.

"Let's take mine," she said.

"OK. Mine can use all the rest it can get."

"Here are the keys. You drive."

"OK."

Sam unlocked the passenger door and let her in. When some women — in fact, most women — get into a low-slung car they look about as graceful as a newborn elephant. But Gena slid in with a combination of two easy movements — first her beautiful behind glided into the bucket seat, then those long lovely legs orchestrated themselves under the dash. She looked up and smiled. Sam twitched.

He closed the door, walked over to his car, unlocked it, pulled down the visor, slid out the derringer, put it into his left coat pocket, and then got into the Ferrari.

"I thought this was pleasure," she said.

"I hope it turns out that way."

"Why do you carry two guns?"

"One doesn't shoot far enough," said Sam. He fired up the Ferrari and headed north on Larchmont.

Neither Gena nor Sam paid any attention to the car parked on the street as they drove by. A man sat in the car. He rubbed his right arm, started the engine, and followed at a discreet distance.

"That's where I live," said Sam, as they passed his apartment house on the 500 block. "Not quite as elegant as your palace in Holmby Hills, but it's handy."

"Oh, I don't live there."

"Why not? There's enough room for the whole Greek Navy."

"But not enough for *two* women."

"Both named Anastas?"

She nodded. "Teresa is a fine person, but —"

"Say, didn't she used to be married to some South American dictator?"

"Yes, he was assassinated in a coup d'etat."

"So she 'flew the coup' — and landed a berth as the Commodore's first mate."

"Second mate. My mother was the first."

Sam turned right on Melrose where Larchmont ended — then left on Gower.

"That used to be the old RKO Studio," said Sam. "It's part of Paramount now. They took down the tower that was on top of that concrete globe up there. More ghosts on the lot than in the cemetery behind it."

"I have the feeling you liked things better as they used to be."

"I have the same feeling. But things change. Hal Roach's studio knocked down; so's Eagle Lion — it's a shopping center now. Twentieth Century on Western's a Zody's — Columbia's vacant — Republic's CBS Television. Hell, none of them even has a gymnasium anymore except Paramount. They can't knock *it* down because it's an official California Historical Monument."

"Really?"

"Yeah. The building was over on Selma and Vine. DeMille shot *The Squaw Man* there. They moved it to Paramount and made it a gym. I used to work out there before —"

"Before what?"

"You know — you're dangerous," said Sam. "Effective as scopolamine."

"What's scopolamine?"

"Never mind."

★ ★ ★

They drove all the way up Hollywood Boulevard past Highland in silence. So did the man in the car following them.

"Where do you want to get that drink?" she asked.

"Anywhere you say. But I'm getting kind of cramped in this sardine can."

"Why don't you park and we'll walk for a while. We'll find a place."

"On Hollywood Boulevard?"

"Don't worry. I'll protect you."

Sam parked the Ferrari and they walked east on Hollywood Boulevard. On the corner of Hollywood and Highland Sam and Gena waited for a light to change. A couple of freaked-out teenage girls approached them.

"Hey," said freaked-out girl number one, "you're a movie star!" She shoved a piece of paper and a pencil at Sam and said, "Give us your autograph."

Sam couldn't refuse such a gracious request so he wrote on the paper and handed it back to her. She looked at the paper, then at Sam. "Hey, you're not Lee Marvin!"

"I'm not? Then who is?"

"Up yours!" said freaked-out girl number one. She tore up the paper and both freaked-out girls walked away.

"You know something?" Gena said.

"What?"

"See this building?"

"Yeah."

"It's First Federal Savings. Did you know that right here on this corner used to be the Hollywood Hotel?"

"You're all right, kid." Sam smiled. "Come on, we got the light."

They crossed the street. In front of John's Pipe Shop Sam said, "We can get a drink at Musso's — it's just —"

"Oh, Sam, look!"

"I'm looking."

"The Wax Museum!"

"I see it."

"You know, I've driven by hundreds of times but I've never been in. Have you?"

"Not since this morning."

"It's still open. Let's go in."

"Sure."

Sam waved at the girl in the box office. "How's business, Indy?"

"Had a good day." The girl smiled. "Getting ready to close up pretty soon."

Sam nodded and guided Gena past the entrance.

"You didn't pay," Gena said.

"I get in free. Come on, let's start with the Chamber of Horrors."

Sam led her down a dank twisting corridor past Frankenstein, the Wolf Man, Dracula, and other children of the night. She squeezed Sam's arm tighter and tighter. He didn't mind a bit.

They came around a corner and almost bumped into a dusky figure wearing a turban and beard. Gena stifled a gasp.

"Hello, Spoony." Sam smiled.

"Sam — welcome back."

"Oh, Miss Anastas — this is Spoony Singh. He owns all this."

"What a beautiful lady." Spoony bowed. "I'd love to do her in wax."

"Some other time, Spoony. We're just taking a quick tour."

"I understand. Enjoy yourselves. Be sure to go through the House of Mirrors. It's our newest attraction."

"We'll do that."

"And Sam. Thank you again for the coat. It adds just the right touch. I should've thought of it myself."

"That's OK."

Spoony stepped back toward the wall and let something drop from his hand. There was a *poof* and a great mushroom of smoke — and Spoony disappeared.

"Quite a showman," said Sam.

"Is he actually an Indian?"

"Bona fidee. Born in Punjab."

"And you really were here this morning?"

"Would *I* lie? Come on." They walked past several wax figures, including Gable, Monroe, Wayne, and Crosby, and came to the House of Mirrors. In front of it was a wax figure of Bogart.

Bogey was wearing a gray felt hat. Both hands were in the pockets of his trench coat. Both pockets had bullet holes and powder burns on them. The left sleeve also had a hole through it.

"You know, Sam," said Gena, "one of these days you *must* tell me what all this is about."

"Maybe I will. One of these days — or nights. Let's go into the House of Mirrors."

They did. The House of Mirrors consisted of a maze of cubicles about three feet square. Not all the walls were mirrored — some were glass, some had figures painted on them. After five or six turns Sam and Gena became separated. They could still catch glimpses of each other — or each other's reflection — from time to time. And they could hear each other.

"Bet you a sinker I beat you out," Sam said loudly.

"What's a sinker?"

"A doughnut."

"You're *on*."

"Don't say that. It's suggestive."

"Maybe I'm suggesting," she teased.

"I'll be out there waiting. And remember what the great poet said."

"What did he say?"

"As you make your way through life Whatever be your goal Keep your eye upon the doughnut And not upon the —"

*"Sam!!!"* she screamed.

Sam saw it just then. Standing in one of the cubicles between them was a figure — not painted — wearing a ski mask and holding a gun with both hands.

The gun went off. One of the glass panels shattered.

"Get down, Gena!" yelled Sam, "and stay down!"

Sam's Luger was already out. He stepped into another cubicle and Ski Mask fired again. More shattered glass.

"You're gonna get yours, dick!" hollered Ski Mask.

"Where's your playmate?" Sam hollered back.

"This one's on me!" Another shot — more shattered glass. Sam fired at the reflection — it was just that — more glass shattered.

Sam moved again. So did Ski Mask.

"You Buster? Or Nero's Uncle?"

"I'm the one you creased last night. The

82

one who's gonna kill you tonight!"

Two shots almost simultaneously — one from Sam, one from Ski Mask. Glass spattered like hail and a piece nicked Sam in the neck.

"What the hell's going on in there?" Sam heard Spoony yell from someplace. "Those mirrors cost me a fortune!"

More of Spoony's fortune went down the drain as Sam's Luger blasted away another panel.

"Damn it to hell! Cut it out!" bellowed Spoony. Nobody paid any attention.

Sam moved forward and hit his head against what turned out to be a plain pane of glass.

"Sonofabitch!" he snapped and moved through another panel. Ski Mask made a dash and he too creamed against a pane of glass. He uttered a much more vile oath and stepped into a panel closer to Sam. Another shot from Ski Mask — followed fast by a blast from Sam's Luger. Another shot apiece — then they moved simultaneously and stood facing each other across the lower half of an already shattered mirror with razor-sharp jagged edges jutting up like stalagmites.

They faced each other for only a fifth of a second — then both men squeezed. Ski Mask's gun went "click." Sam's gun went "bang." And Ski Mask fell forward onto the craggy spine of glass.

It was relatively easy for Sam and Gena to find their way out of the House of Mirrors — there wasn't much of a house left.

Spoony was waiting by the figure of Bogart when Sam and Gena came out. "Sam, for the love of heaven! Do you know how much those mirrors cost?"

"Don't look at me, Spoony. He shot first."

"Oh, Sam, Sam darling." Gena put her arms around him, then pulled back and touched his neck with long soft fingers. "You're bleeding."

"Not as much as him." Sam pointed his Luger at the mess inside. "Spoony, call Lieutenant Bumbera at Homicide. Tell him what happened, but don't stand too close to the phone."

"All right, Sam — look!"

There was a bullet hole through Bogey's gray felt hat.

"What're you worried about?" said Sam. "I'll get him another hat."

# 12

Bumbera, Hacksaw, and company were there in ten minutes. This time they managed to keep the newspaper boys out of it — Spoony's call had been directly to the Lieutenant.

The police officers listened to Gena and Sam's story, as verified by Spoony. The basket boys managed to scoop up Ski Mask and cart the remains away. Nobody recognized what was left of his face.

Sam succeeded in persuading Bumbera to allow Gena to leave. It wasn't all that hard when Bumbera realized who she was — or who her father was. They all agreed to keep her out of it. One of the officers escorted Gena to her car.

For some reason Sgt. Horace Hacksaw's hackles were up. "I think you're some kind of a nut," he said to Sam.

"Gee whiz, Horace. I think you're the berries."

"And I don't like those smart remarks. How'd you like to have your face done over again?"

"How'd you like a Scotch and soda?" Sam smiled.

"Hack —" Bumbera put his hand on the Sergeant's sleeve.

"Well, what kind of a nut is he?" Hacksaw said. "Going around in that get-up and with that face!"

"Any law against a man having a face like that?" Bumbera asked.

"It ain't natural. He's a psycho."

"Take it easy, Hack. Look, Sam, these killings got to stop. What're you trying to do?"

"Improve the breed."

"What the hell are you talking about?"

"When I get through there'll be better — but fewer — criminals around for you cops to worry about."

"You see, Bummy," Hacksaw exploded, "he's nuts! I got half a mind . . ."

"That's about all you got," Sam said.

"Cut it out! Both of you!"

"Then tell this ape to lay off! What the hell does he expect me to do when these hoods come after me with cannons? Am I supposed to tell 'em to wait till I call the police? Or should I let 'em shoot me and my clients full of lead?"

"You've got a right to defend yourself."

"Oh," Sam sneered, "is that still the law?"

"You know it is."

"Then tell it to your friend, the ape man."

"Sam, sometimes you go too far," Bumbera said softly.

"And sometimes too far — isn't far enough!"

"Sam, just give me your word you're not holding back anything we ought to know."

"You got it."

"All right. You have a car here?"

"No, it's at the office."

"I'll drive you to it."

"Drop me off at the apartment. I'll walk to work in the morning. I need the exercise."

"Sure. Say Sam, don't you ever just *wound* anybody?"

"Yeah, I nicked that guy last night — and look what happened — he got mad."

It was almost one in the A.M. when Bumbera dropped Sam off. The night was windless and warm and quiet except for a dog barking in some backyard. From another yard another dog answered.

Sam got out of Bumbera's car and closed the door. "Thanks for the lift, copper."

"Sure. Say, Sam, you like being a detective?"

"It's a living — so far."

"Don't you miss — ?"

"Look, Bummy, either book me or let me

go to bed. Who needs this curbside third degree?"

"Sure — sure," said Bumbera, the way Garfield used to. "Good night, shamus."

"Good night, sweetheart."

Sam walked into the apartment house. The dogs were still talking to each other. From the way the conversation was going now, one had to be a boy dog — and the other a girl dog.

As Sam started to undress he took another gander at Horst Borsht's riddle. After a couple of minutes he decided it had been a long enough day. He'd sleep on it tonight and riddle the riddle tomorrow — or try. He lifted the knob off the post of his brass bed — made the letter into a tube — slipped it into the post and replaced the knob. He finished undressing, went to the bathroom, took a cold shower, and slipped into his pajama bottoms, then went into the living room to turn off the light. Then he heard it.

A knock. Then another. Then another.

Holy — holy — Toledo — Toledo?!?! Could it be?

It was.

Her face had that same "Isabel" look she tempted Tyrone Power with in *The Razor's Edge.*

Sam didn't need tempting.

"We haven't had that drink yet." She

smiled her Isabel smile.

"Are you kidding?"

"Would *I* kid you? Found a liquor store that was open." She held out a sack. "How do you like your brandy?"

"In bed."

"Sam."

"Are you coming in — or am I coming out?"

"I'd better come in. You're not dressed for hallways."

"And you're not dressed for bed," he said.

"Shall we compromise in the kitchen?" She glided in and he pushed the door shut.

"Would you settle for the sofa?" he said.

Gena lifted the bottle from the sack. "Grand Marnier. Do you like oranges?"

"If they're from your tree."

"You've got a good physique, Mr. Marlow."

"And you ain't exactly the Hunchback of Notre Dame. I'll get a couple of snifters while you uncork."

He came back with two water glasses and poured three fingers of Grand Marnier into each.

"What'll we drink to?" She smiled.

"To beauty — and truth —"

She nodded.

"— and things that go bump in the night," he added.

They drank. By now the dogs were howling at each other from their respective backyards.

They sat on the sofa. Each took another sip — then they both put their glasses down on the coffee table. He turned her gently so her body came across his chest, facing him. Sam kissed her and she kissed back.

It was still the prelude but more instruments had joined the orchestra. The music was warmer and sweeter — a hundred violins quivered, and so did they. She eased away and touched his lips with her fingertips — she had a way of doing it — sensual, tender, and titillating. He started to draw her closer again.

"Sam," she whispered, and withdrew — but not really. "Give me a few minutes to get ready."

She rose. Not fast, not slow. Like royalty in perfect command of the ceremony. She poured more brandy into each glass. There was even something regal — but suggestive — about the way she handled the bottle and poured the amber liquid into those plain kitchen glasses. She transformed them into crystal stemware fashioned for the wedding night of a prince and his bride.

She took her crystal goblet and walked toward the bedroom.

"I'll knock three times," he said.

There are walks and there are walks. When

Duchess walked she held nothing back — like Marilyn Monroe, she gave it all she had. There was little left to the imagination. The weight shifted like balloons filled with liquid from one side of her rear to the other.

But Gena's walk: it was supple, but not as fluid. As if she were holding something back — unreleased, unused in reserve — private yet provocative and promising.

To Sam it seemed like twelve years till she got to the bedroom and closed the door. And it only took twelve eternities for the next two minutes to tick away. More time than in all the calendars ever made.

After walking around the world a few times Sam drank the three fingers of brandy. He poured in three more, took the glass and bottle, and walked to the bedroom door. Softly he knocked — once — twice — three times.

He turned the knob — and went in.

She was in the big brass bed. Her beautiful face and hair easily rested against the pillow propped on the headboard.

The thin, soft sheet outlined her nakedness. It coursed gently over and around every edge and curve of her sinuous body, flowed and followed every valley and upland, every sweep and bend. Only her arms, long and pliant and alabaster-white, were outside the sheet. She raised them invitingly to Sam.

He went to her, put the bottle and glass on the nightstand, and sat on the bed. Her arms moved smoothly behind his shoulders and brought him closer until their lips nearly touched — nearly — as ever so slowly and gently and expertly her fingers glided with just the slightest friction across his back and neck, working like ten tiny tingling vibrators. And just as Sam's mouth touched hers, barely tasting the sweet brandy, she moved her hands to his face.

"Sam," she whispered. And turned her head away slightly.

Her hand went to the edge of the sheet that still covered her. She took it between her thumb and two fingers and raised it — not fast, not slow, almost like a stage curtain — until she was naked before him.

No other living thing had ever been so perfect and so beautiful.

The prelude was over; the cymbals clashed and the symphony started. It was all the music ever played — all the love songs ever written — birds on the wing — the beat beat beat of the tom-toms — till the end of time — something to remember you by — Sunday, Monday, or always — dancing in the dark — I've got you under my skin. It was Gilbert and Garbo, Gable and Garson, Tracy and Hepburn, Ladd and Lake, Bogart and Bacall. It was Samson and Delilah, Napoleon and Josephine, Romeo and Juliet.

It tasted of almonds and gunmetal — of Hersheys and iodine — of white wine and salt water. It was higher than the highest mountain and deeper than the deep blue sea. It was the soft echolalia of the surf, the frenetic whine of an air-raid siren. It was the Song of Solomon and the devil's damnedest. It was in and out — up and down — over and around — a left hook to the jaw — a massage. It was a knife in the gut, a nurse in the night, head in the sand and season in the sun — fluff and fury, oil on troubled waters, and then the blast from a stick of dynamite.

It was over. For now. One last sweet kiss and it was over for now.

They lay beside each other in the dark — arms touching. Silent.

"Sam," she said finally, "why are all those people trying to kill you?"

"It's their job, I guess."

"And what's your job?"

"To kill 'em first, I guess."

"You know, I'll come into an awful lot of money one day."

"Congratulations."

"It would be nice if you're still around to help me spend some of it."

"*Very* nice."

"I'd consider it a favor."

"OK. I'm still on retainer."

"Oh, I don't think so. I'd say we're all square."

"Uh-uh. I don't accept money for —"

"I mean for getting Bumbera to let me leave and helping —"

"Oh, that."

"I like your style, Sam."

"I like your perfume, lady."

"I'm glad you didn't see those pictures."

"Let's skip that part. Get some sleep."

She kissed him and pulled up the sheet. They were both asleep in the next two minutes — arms still touching.

Two hours later Sam woke. Gena wasn't lying next to him. She was sitting on the side of the bed.

"What're you doing, Princess?"

"Looking at you."

"Can't you think of anything better to do?"

"Maybe. Can you?"

He put his hands behind her naked back and brought her down.

# 13

It was after eight in the morning when they woke again. They showered together. Then Sam shaved while Gena made coffee and poured orange juice.

Sam dressed, took Horst Borsht's letter out of the bedpost, put it in his inside pocket, and went to the kitchen. They had breakfast. At 9:15 Gena drove him to the corner of Larchmont and Beverly.

"If you don't call me," she said, "I'm going to call you."

"Either way," he smiled, "it'll be too long."

"Sam, I enjoyed the drink."

"Not as much as I did." He squeezed out of the Ferrari and waved as she pulled away.

The blind newsman handed Sam another free paper. "Cryin' out loud, Sam," he said, "at this rate there won't be any bad guys left."

"Yeah — what a pity."

Sam walked up the stairway. About half a dozen ladies from the gymnasium were clustered there gawking and giggling. Mother poked her head out just as Sam hit the landing.

"Did you find Nicky yet?"

"Hot on his trail."

"Humph," she snorted. "Are you *sure* you're a detective?"

Sam winked at her.

"Find him!"

"Yes, Mother."

Sam opened the door to his outer office. Duchess was leaning low over an open drawer of a filing cabinet, filing her lunch. The skirt came right about to where her underwear would've been. Sam's lip twitched.

"Good morning, Duchess."

"Oh, Sam! You startled me!"

"And vice versa."

"You sure are getting a lot of free pub in the papers."

"Yeah, pretty soon we won't have to advertise."

"Shooting all those guys — aren't you running out of ammunition?"

"Thanks for reminding me."

"Just part of my duties." She twittered and walked across the room, holding nothing back. Sam waited until she sat, then went into his office.

He called Bumbera. Bumbera was in. Sam asked what the R and I boys had found out about Nero's Uncle.

"His name was Joe Kargo, among a lot of

other AKAs — a cheap hoodlum for hire with a long string of arrests and two convictions for assault."

"Thanks, Bummy. And thanks again for keeping the lady out of it."

"Hell, that's all right. Who needs pressure from her old man? That guy's got a lot of juice."

"That ain't all he's got."

"Sam, you sure you're not holding anything back?"

"All I know is what I read in the papers."

"Yeah, well, see if you can stay out of the papers tomorrow. You know, one of these days that could be *you* in one of those cold compartments."

"Everybody dies."

"Ain't it the truth. Did you get any sleep last night?"

"No, I stayed up with the late show. So long, sweetheart."

As he hung up, Duchess ambled into the office. "Newspaper men have been calling. They want a statement from you."

"What did you tell 'em?"

"I told them you were still out, but they're going to call back. What'll I say?"

"Say I'm out still."

"And there's a man here to see you. He's a driver."

"Truck? Or bus?"

"Limousine, from the looks of him."

"Send him in, but tell him to leave the car in your office."

"Si-si." She started to amble out but stopped at the door. "No, Sam, he didn't bring his car up. Just his uniform."

"In that case, send him and his uniform in."

The fellow came in, uniform and all. "I am Turhan."

"Sure you are."

He was as thin as he was dark. He also had some kind of an accent. "I was instructed to deliver this to you, *effendi*." He held out a blue envelope. Sam took it.

"Done and done."

"I was instructed to wait."

"For how long?"

"Until you respond, *effendi*."

"Well, that shouldn't take too long," said Sam, tearing open the envelope. "Say, Turhan, you getting enough to eat?"

Turhan merely nodded — in a slightly snotty way, Sam thought. There was a blue letter in the blue envelope and a green five-hundred-dollar bill in the blue letter.

"Such a lot of money around here lately," Sam remarked. He read the letter. A name was engraved across the top of the blue stationery.

MUSTAFA HAKIM
I would appreciate an hour of your time.

                                                    M.H.

"Well, the price is right. Which hour does whats-his-name want?"

"The next, if it is convenient."

Sam snapped the five hundred between his two hands. "President McKinley makes it convenient. Where does this —" Sam looked at the letter again "— Mustafa Hakim hole up?"

Turhan looked perplexed. "Excuse me, *effendi*. I do not comprehend."

"Where does ol' Mustafa live?"

"He is stopping at the Beverly Hills Hotel."

"Oh, I thought he'd be at the Garden of Allah."

"Excuse me, *effendi?*"

"OK, OK. I'll drive over."

"My instructions were to drive you."

"Look, Turhan, I'm a big boy now. Even take baths all alone — I don't need anybody to wipe my nose or drive me anyplace. Tell him I'll be poolside in half an hour. He can page me."

"As you wish, *effendi.*"

"Say, what kind of lingo is that 'effendi' stuff?"

"In Turkey *effendi* is a term of respect, sir."

"Oh, are you a turkey?"

"I am a Turkish citizen."

"Yeah? Well, I've smoked some of your cigarettes. They're real lung cloggers."

"Thank you, *effendi*."

Turhan backed and bowed his way out of the office and Duchess bounced her way in. "I'm going down for a doughnut. Want one?" she gaily inquired.

"No, thanks." Sam yawned.

"I guess you didn't sleep so good last night."

"I ain't complaining."

"Killing those people — don't that lay on your mind?"

"*Lay* on my mind?" Sam asked.

"Yeah, don't you see their faces in your dreams?"

"I only dream about you — and other girls."

"I dream about banana splits. Wake up in the middle of the night just dying for a banana split." She sighed.

"They're naked."

"The banana splits?"

"No, the girls I dream about."

"Now, Sam." Duchess shook her finger, but somehow her whole blouse bounced. "Naughty, naughty!"

Sam folded the five hundred and put it in his pants pocket.

"Well, time to shove off."

"Where you going?"

"Lunch."

"So early?"

"In New York it's way past noon. By the way, they did a good job on both of them."

"Both of what?"

"Your legs. They look real waxy. I didn't know they went up that high."

"My legs?"

"No, the wax. So long, Duchess."

# 14

Sam had memorized Horst Borsht's limerick. He had read and reread, worked and reworked it, at least a thousand times. He kept repeating it out loud as he drove toward the Beverly Hills Hotel. The more he said it the screwier it sounded. To hell with it. He turned on the car radio, tuned to KFI, and listened to Dick Whitington, who made about as much sense as Horst Borsht's riddle. Sam turned the dial over to KPOL, where an orchestra was playing "Something To Remember You By."

Sam remembered the song as the theme from *Mr. Lucky*, RKO, 1943. Cary Grant, Laraine Day, Charles Bickford and Paul Stewart. That Grant. What style! No man ever glided more gracefully across the screen. Well-groomed, too. Still, he could be tough. When he took the roll of dimes in his fist and put the slug on that hood, you believed it. And what about Grant with Victor McLagen and Douglas Fairbanks, Jr., in *Gunga Din*? They just don't make pictures like that anymore — or people.

Sam took a right at the Beverly Hills Hotel driveway and pulled to a stop by the porte cochere. There were a couple of uniformed attendants on duty. Neither seemed overly anxious to park the Plymouth. They whispered to each other and finally one nodded and came over. He looked startled when he saw Sam's face. Sam gave him a twitch and walked up the porte cochere, through the lobby and out to the pool.

He drew the usual strange looks from the few people in and around the swimming hole. They were mostly New Yorkers here on business, some with their wives and most of them in the television business — network executives and agency people. About half of them were doing the Bloody Mary bit. One fellow sat facing the sun, holding a creased sheet of silvery tinfoil to his face with both hands — trying to get an instant suntan before going back to New York.

"Mr. Marlow," said a lady's voice. Sam turned toward it. Yes, the voice came from a lady, all right. "Mr. Hakim sent me."

"That was friendly of him."

She was tall and blond and perfect — almost too perfect. Her hair couldn't really have been that perfect a shade of blond. And her nose — that was too perfect, too.

"He is waiting in the bungalow." Even her

speech was too perfect. Sam couldn't help wondering how perfect she'd be in bed.

"I am Cynthia Ashley."

"How do."

She started walking. So did Sam.

"And *what* do you do, Cyn, my dear, besides fetch for Mr. Whats-his-name?"

"I am Mr. Hakim's executive secretary."

"Yeah? How's your shorthand?"

She smiled. A perfect smile.

"Does your boss spend a lot of time here in L.A.?" Sam asked.

"No. We travel extensively."

"We *do*, huh?"

"But Mr. Hakim maintains a bungalow at the hotel."

"Doesn't everybody?"

And there was Turhan standing skinny in front of one of the bungalows. It was painted blue.

"This must be the place," said Sam. "Hello, Turhan. How're they hangin'?"

Turhan didn't know what Sam was talking about. Cynthia Ashley, executive secretary, did — but her perfect face never changed expression.

She unlocked and opened the door of the bungalow and bade Sam enter. He did and she followed.

Everything in the room was done in blue —

everything. Carpeting, drapery, lamps, furniture — everything. One of the blue doors that connected to another blue room opened and a man walked in.

"So good of you to come," said Mustafa Hakim.

"I couldn't resist your invitation — the green one."

Mustafa Hakim looked like Zachary Scott in *The Mask of Dimitrios*, except for one thing. He was all done in blue too. His suit, shirt, tie, diamond ring, cuff links, socks, and shoes . . . blue. His eyes were blue, his hair had a bluish tint, and so did his complexion. Maybe it was just a reflection from the room or maybe it was some sort of skin disease — but damn if he didn't look blue.

Hakim glanced back into the room he had just come from. "Mr. Zinderneuf, won't you join us?"

Another man walked into the parlor. He didn't exactly walk — he marched. This guy was a ringer for Lionel Atwill, right down to a wooden arm ol' Atwill had in *Son of Frankenstein* — even wore a black glove on the fake hand.

"Mr. Marlow," Hakim said, "this is Wolf Zinderneuf." Wolf Zinderneuf clicked his heels with a loud report.

Sam clicked his heels right back, but with

no sound. It's not easy to click heels on a blue carpet two inches thick. It takes a lot of practice.

"May I offer you a drink, Mr. Marlow?" Mustafa Hakim spoke flawless English.

"Got a beer?"

"Certainly. Mr. Zinderneuf, the usual?"

"Bourbon."

That figured, Sam thought. The executive secretary was already at the blue sideboard-refrigerator doing the bartending.

"Say, what kind of a name is Hakim?" Sam asked. "Greek? There seem to be an awful lot of Greeks around lately."

Hakim's blue eyes narrowed.

"Hardly Greek. I am Turkish. You may be aware that the Greeks and the Turks have a long history of — shall I say — incompatibility?"

"If that's what you want to say, it's OK with me. Where'd you get those baby blues? I've seen Greeks with blue eyes, never Turks."

"My mother was not Turkish."

"That's a coincidence. Neither was mine."

"Mr. Marlow, I believe in coming directly to the point."

"That's a good policy — usually."

"So much precious time is wasted in this world."

"Yeah, well, my time's not all that precious.

106

Thanks, Cyn," he said. She had walked over, carrying a tray. Sam took the bottle of Heineken's and the frosted glass. Cynthia Ashley then went over to Zinderneuf. Wolf grabbed the glass of bourbon with his good right hand and clicked his heels.

"Thank you, Cynthia," said Hakim. It obviously was an expression of dismissal more than appreciation. She smiled, set down the empty tray, and walked out the front door.

"Isn't the exec sec in on this?" Sam inquired.

"Up to a point." Hakim smiled.

Sam held up the beer glass. "Aren't you having something cool?"

"I rarely drink or smoke."

"Yeah? What's your outlook on sex — with women?"

Mustafa Hakim chuckled politely.

"Why, you dirty old man," Sam said. "OK, it's your five hundred. What can I do for you?"

"Mr. Marlow, you'll find very quickly that I am a candid man. Straight to the point. Have you ever heard of the Eyes of Alexander?"

"I'm pretty candid myself. The answer is yes."

"Good. Very good. I can see we'll get along."

"Up to a point." Sam took another swig of beer.

"You are acquainted with the history of the Eyes?"

"Not really. I know that they were part of a statue once and are worth quite a bit of money."

"That, sir, may be the understatement of the ages."

"Well, that's about all I know. Why don't you fill me in?"

"Volumes could be written on the subject." Hakim smiled. "I'll summarize briefly. Very briefly."

"Can I get another beer while you do?"

"Please — my house is your house."

Sam went to the sideboard-refrigerator. "Say, you got any American beer? This stuff tastes greenish to me."

"I believe so."

There were several bottles of Budweiser next to the Heineken's. Sam picked up a Bud, twisted off the cap, and drank from the bottle while Mustafa Hakim spoke and Wolf Zinderneuf stood at attention.

"In 344 B.C. Alexander of Macedon, who was to be known in history as Alexander the Great, won a brilliant victory over the Persian army of Darius at Granicus near the sea of Marmora in Asia Minor. Among the Persian dead were Arbupales, grandson of Artaxerxes; Spithridates, satrap of Lydia; Mithrobuzanes,

108

governor of Cappadocia; Mithridates, son-in-law of Darius, —"

"Hold it!" said Sam. "Could you skip the names and stick with the facts?"

"Indeed. To commemorate the victory at Granicus, Alexander commissioned a bust of himself, to be sculpted by Aristopholos. The eyes of the statue were to be the two most perfectly matched natural blue sapphires in the world. The bust was soon finished but the search for the sapphires went on for years — nearly ten years.

"Finally, in 323 B.C., Aristopholos and Alexander were satisfied that the two most perfect gems in the world had been found. One of the sapphires came from Ceylon, the other from Kashmir. But by then Alexander lay on his deathbed in Babylon. According to legend, the bust with the blue sapphire eyes was the last thing on earth Alexander ever saw. But his death was only the beginning of the history of the statue. Alexander's empire was divided into four parts: Syria and Babylonia under Seleucus, Egypt under Ptolemy, Thrace and Asia Minor under Lysimachus, Macedonia and Greece under Cassander.

"For reasons unrecorded the statue went with Ptolemy and reposed in a palace at Alexandria. I will not detail its sojourns in the ensuing centuries, but at various times the bust, still intact, became part of the spoils of a succession of conquerors — Romans, Celts, Gauls, Huns, —"

At the word "Huns" Wolf Zinderneuf stood even a little straighter.

"— Franks, Ottomans. Finally, after nearly two thousand years, the statue found its way back to Asia Minor, not far from the site of the Battle of Granicus. It was now in the possession of Ali Pasha.

"During the War of 1821 between Greece and Turkey a band of Greek renegades, with the help of Russian Orthodox allies, succeeded in stealing the statue from Istanbul and smuggling it into Greece. There it remained for 120 years, until the Germans invaded Greece."

"Yeah," said Sam, "now we're getting into some history even I can remember."

"Have you ever been to Greece, Mr. Marlow?"

"Can't say I have."

"There's not much to be said for the land itself — the waters around the islands, however, are the bluest in the world."

"That so?"

"Mr. Zinderneuf has spent some time in Greece . . . during the war."

"That so?"

"Yes!" said Zinderneuf from between rat-thin lips.

"He talks!" said Sam.

"Certainly," said Zinderneuf. Even one word at a time, his accent came through thick as cold molasses. Just like Otto Preminger.

"I'd wager," said Sam, "that when Wolfie here was in Greece he wasn't wearing blue. I'd wager it was gray. With a crooked cross on an armband."

"Mr. Zinderneuf had the distinction of being the third youngest general in the German Army during the Second World War."

"Is that so?"

Zinderneuf clicked again.

"General Zinderneuf was one of the officers in charge of the Army of Occupation," Hakim went on. "A Greek partisan not immune to pain told General Zinderneuf about the statue, which was then hidden in the catacombs of a monastery just outside the city of Athens. The fortunes of battle had already changed; Zinderneuf managed to secure the bust, render it to bits and pieces, remove the sapphires, and secrete them in a safe hiding place only hours prior to the Allied takeover. The General was severely wounded and suffered the loss of his left arm. He was captured — later tried and convicted as a —"

Hakim cleared his throat and glanced at Zinderneuf — "war criminal."

"How long were you in the slammer, Wolfie?"

"More than seventeen years," Zinderneuf said with tight lips.

"Hell, that's longer than the Third Reich lasted."

"To get back to the sapphires —" Hakim said.

"Yeah, let's."

"In 1963, subsequent to his release, Zinderneuf returned to Greece to secure possession of the hidden gems. It was then and there he came across a relative of his — a nephew who had served under him during the Occupation. The nephew had gone to America and become involved in motion pictures, and was working on an American film being shot partially in Greece."

"I'll bet you a cold beer the nephew was a prop man."

"Correct."

"And with the unlikely name of Horst Borsht."

"Correct again. Zinderneuf trusted his nephew implicitly."

"Yeah, the two of them were probably getting ready for World War III." Sam drank more beer.

"Because of Zinderneuf's record he was afraid of being watched and knew he would have a difficult time smuggling the sapphires out of Greece."

"But Horst Borsht wouldn't."

"Boxes and boxes of items were brought in to be used on the film —"

"— and those boxes and boxes would leave the country so the rest of the picture could be shot back in the States."

"Correct again."

"And Horst Borsht could hide the sapphires in one of those boxes and boxes."

"That was the plan."

"And it worked?"

"Up to a point. Borsht and the sapphires left Greece — unfortunately, Mr. Zinderneuf did not, not until much later — more than a dozen years later."

"That just about brings us up to date. What detained Wolfie?"

"He was recognized by one of the Greeks from the Occupation. An argument ensued — first, name-calling, then violence. Mr. Zinderneuf stabbed the Greek in the throat with a fork."

"Back in the slammer!"

"Correct." Mustafa Hakim smiled. Wolf Zinderneuf didn't.

"And all this time," said Sam, "Horst

113

Borsht is sitting on those hot rocks back in the good old U.S.A."

"Until his recent, unfortunate demise."

"Yeah. By the way, did you fellas pay for the demising?"

"Definitely not."

"About those sapphires — ol' Borsht couldn't take 'em with him, could he?"

"Definitely not."

"And you boys haven't got 'em. I know — 'definitely not.' Well, that's a pretty good yarn you spin, Mr. Hakim. Now how about I ask you a few 'how comes'?"

"Go right ahead."

"How come you're involved in the caper?"

"Just prior to his release Mr. Zinderneuf made contact with me, asking if I would be interested in bidding on the Eyes with a certain other collector — once the authenticity of the sapphires was verified."

"And you *were* interested."

"That is why I am here. Unfortunately, Mr. Borsht's demise changes the picture."

"Yeah, unfortunately for you *and* him. I'll bet another beer the 'other collector' isn't a Turk."

"You win again. Now, may I inquire — are you currently in the employ of the Commodore? You see, I am very candid."

"The answer is that I am not — currently.

I'm just an independent businessman trying to get more independent."

"A good answer. *Very* good."

"Glad you like it."

"What about *Miss* Borsht?"

"What *about* Miss Borsht?"

"Are you working for her?"

"Sorta — not exclusive."

"Does she know about the sapphires?"

"No."

"Are you certain?"

"Yes. She would've told me."

"We thought so. Mr. Marlow, I am prepared to pay you the sum of one hundred thousand dollars."

"Who do I have to shoot?"

"Hopefully, no one. Bring me the Eyes of Alexander. One hundred thousand dollars."

"Yeah. I heard the figure the first time. Where does Zinderneuf come in?"

"We have since made our own arrangement."

"Partnering against the Commodore . . ."

"Let's say pooling our resources."

"Can't be a whole hell of a lot of resources — or you wouldn't need me."

"What is your answer?" Hakim smiled.

"I'll need some time —"

"Certainly."

"— to think it over. You really don't like Greeks?"

"That is not always the case. As a matter of fact, Anastas and I were business partners a long time ago. We owned our first freighter together."

"What happened to the partnership?"

"It was dissolved when he saw fit to scuttle our ship for insurance so he could go into business for himself."

"Well, it seems like both you boys've done all right."

"You might say that."

"I just did. And what about you — you think you got your five hundred dollars' worth?"

"That is merely a token payment. Bring me the Eyes —"

"Yeah, I know — one hundred thousand dollars. I'll tell you this. It's the best offer I've had so far."

"Very good."

"I think." Sam moved to the door. "Say, Wolfie, did you know Zinderneuf was the name of the fort where everybody got killed in *Beau Geste*?"

"Yes." Zinderneuf clicked.

"Incidentally, Mr. Marlow," Mustafa Hakim asked, "just how many men have *you* killed?"

"Just as many as were trying to kill me. By the way, Mr. Hakim — what's your favorite color?"

"Blue." Hakim smiled.

"I kinda thought so. I suppose that's why you want the sapphires — they *are* blue, aren't they?"

"The most perfect blue in the world."

"Yeah. Say, when did you and Wolfie get into town?"

"Late last night."

"Uh huh. Well, thanks for the beer."

As Sam reached for the door there was a soft knock. The key turned, the door opened, and standing there next to Cynthia Ashley with an astonished look on his face was Mr. Zebra, smelling of lavender.

"Come in," said Mustafa Hakim. "Mr. Marlow was just leaving. Mr. Marlow, this is Mr. Zebra."

"Pleased to meet you, Mr. Marlow," said Mr. Zebra in a shaky, anguished voice.

"Likewise," said Sam as he went out the door.

# 15

When the hotel parking attendant brought the Plymouth to the porte cochere Sam tipped him a fiver just to see the expression on his face. It wasn't worth it.

But Sam was feeling flush. People were shoving money at him from all directions. All he had to do was figure out how to find the Eyes of Alexander — *and* who would try to kill him next. And when. And where. Of course, a lot of other people were trying to find the sapphires too. But they didn't have possession of Horst Borsht's letter. Only he did . . . for all the good it had done him so far. He'd have to get around to telling Bumbera about it sooner or later. Later, he decided.

Sam drove past Chasen's on Beverly Boulevard and headed east toward Larchmont. The drive gave him an opportunity to go over the plot — or plots — and the cast of characters, in order of appearance so far. There were Mother, her cat, and Nicky. They probably had nothing to do with the sapphires. Then there was Elsa, with Buster and Nero's Uncle. Scratch Nero's Uncle from the scenario.

Horst Borsht, another scratch — and Joe Kargo, ditto. Lt. Marion Bumbera and Sgt. Horace Hacksaw — Sam would no doubt see more of them, plenty more than he wanted to see of Hacksaw.

Ah, Gena — the leading lady of the piece. Maybe she fit in with the sapphires and maybe not. There were other places she fit just swell. Then there were Petey Cane, jock, and Ralph the torpedo. Sam was pretty sure he'd seen the last of them. But George with the swinging sap — he was bound to make a return appearance in the libretto.

Commodore Alexander Anastas — the old fox. He hadn't even mentioned the sapphires, but he sure as hell knew about them. And Mrs. Anastas — the fugitive from the coup. Who knew what she knew? There was the oily, perfumed Mr. Zebra — he'd have some explaining to do when next they met.

Then Turhan, the skinny, and Cynthia Ashley, the perfect. Sam wondered if he'd ever find out how perfect she was. But nobody could be as perfect as Gena. He could still feel her all over him.

Getting back to the characters: there were just two more. Mustafa Hakim, the blue Turkish delight, and Wolf Zinderneuf, the Nazi who'd done more time than the Bird Man of Alcatraz. Then one more came to mind. Somebody had been parked outside Horst Borsht's house — the horn honker who was out there waiting for something, and not for what happened. Horn honker could be one of the above characters or somebody in the wings watching and listening for his cue to make an entrance again.

Well, that seemed to round out the dramatis personae. All he had to do was sort out the good guys from the bad guys. Damned few looked especially good. In fact, most of them would probably slice up a close relative for a chance at the two blue baubles.

For some reason, thinking about baubles made him think of Duchess. If she didn't quit with those short skirts and no brassiere and start with some underwear, Sam would go bananas around the office. He had sex on the brain too much lately anyhow — if that was possible. It was, for a detective who wanted to stay alert — and alive.

When Sam got back to his office Duchess was having lunch. She had gone downstairs and gotten three scoops of ice cream, taken the two bananas out of the sack from the filing cabinet, and made herself a banana split in a bowl she kept in her desk.

"Dibs," said Sam when he walked in.

"Dibs? Who's that?" Duchess asked.

"Dibs isn't a who, it's a what."

"Well then, I don't know *what* dibs is."

"We used to say dibs when we were kids. It means I'd like some of your banana split."

"Oh." Duchess licked her lips and held out the bowl with the spoon in it. "Help yourself."

Sam took a spoonful of ice cream. "Thanks."

"Is that all you want?" She had a way of saying things like that that sounded provocative.

"Yeah, I just needed a chaser for the beer."

Duchess smiled even though she didn't know what Sam was talking about. He smiled back.

"Any calls?"

"A bunch of them, including the underwear people. They'd still like to see you. Oh, and the guy who talks dirty called again. I wrote down most of what he said. You know, Sam, I think he's got a problem. Just listen to this . . ."

"Duchess, why do you bother to write that stuff down?"

"Well, I can't remember it."

"Then forget it." Sam took the paper and tore it down and across.

"OK. But I still think he needs help."

"Not from you — or me."

"You're the boss."

"Thanks. Did Elsa call?"

"Nope."

"Thanks again." Sam went into his office. As he got to his desk Duchess buzzed him and said that Gena Anastas was on the phone. Did Sam want to talk to her? He did.

"Hello, Angel."

"Sam," she said, "I'm still thinking about last night."

"I'm thinking about the next night."

"When? Tonight?"

"I hope so, but I'll have to call you. A few things've come up."

"Blonds, brunettes, or redheads?"

"Business."

"Why don't you retire?"

"I'm looking forward to it."

"So am I," she laughed. "Bye."

Sam called Elsa at home: no answer. He got the Hollywood Bowl office number and talked to her — small talk. He wanted to ask her about the sapphires, but not on the phone. He said he'd stop by the house after she got home from work.

Then he put a call in to Mr. Zebra's answering service and left word for Mr. Zebra to call him. While he was still on the phone Duchess came into the room, licking ice cream and banana from her luscious lips.

"There's a man on the other line — says it's

urgent he talk to you."

Sam mashed the other phone button. "Sam Marlow," he said.

"Do you want to know where the Eyes are?" The voice was muffled by a handkerchief or something.

"That'd be nice," said Sam as casually as he could.

"There's a garage down the alley from you — behind the Vanity Fair building. The door will be unlocked. Come alone in five minutes. Don't bring any guns — or no deal." He hung up.

"I'll be damned," said Sam.

"What's the matter?" Duchess asked. "Did he talk dirty?"

"I don't know — yet."

"See. You should've wrote it down like I do."

Sam rose. "I got to go."

"Where?"

Sam put the Luger in his desk drawer. "See a man about a couple of rocks." Sam took a hit from the office bottle and twitched.

"Sam, aren't you gonna take your gun?"

"No — keep an eye on it for me."

"I'm afraid of those things."

"You're supposed to be. Duchess — there's something on your chin."

Duchess's rosy tongue went after it and got

it. "Banana," she said. "Thanks."

Mother poked her head out the door.
"What about Nicky?"
"He's definitely alive."
"What about his shirts and shorts?"
"What about them?"
"You were going to look through them."
"No need to. I'm zeroing in on him."
"I'll zero in on him, all right," she huffed.
"That's what he's afraid of," Sam mumbled.
"You said what?"
"I said that's what love is made of."
She slammed the door shut.

Sam walked south down the alley between
Larchmont and Lucerne, past the rear entrances of the Crocker Bank, the health food
store, the Security Bank, and Jurgensen's, almost to the end of the narrow passageway.
And there was the garage. Sam peered
through the small window on the side door —
dark as the inside of a whale's belly. All he
could see was the dim outline of an automobile. He went around the back and tried the
double-door lift: locked. He walked to the
side door again and turned the knob. The
door gave. Sam pushed it open and cautiously
took a step inside, trying to get his eyes to ad-

just to the darkness. They did — but to a different kind of darkness.

Even as it happened, in the tenth of a second it took to take effect, Sam knew it was a karate chop that hit him. A *shuto* blow with the edge of a hand, the meaty, fleshy part — but it wasn't very meaty or fleshy. It was harder than the roll of dimes Cary Grant used in *Mr. Lucky*. And it was a left hand, but that didn't mean the blow giver was left-handed — a lot of karate commandos preferred the left hand. It's looser, faster, and less tense because they don't use it as much as the right hand. Sam thought about all that in the tenth of a second — all that and more.

The blow from the karate chop felt different from the one from the sap — sharper, more penetrating. The blow giver had aimed right at the hairline and hit his mark. Sam hit the cement floor thinking just one more thought — what a horse's ass he was. Then nothing.

It took the horse's ass about ten minutes to come to. He wasn't lying on his face where he'd fallen. Sam was on his back, and in spite of the tambourine he was wearing for a head, he knew why.

As he lay there Sam managed to creep his right hand across his chest until it reached his inside pocket — the empty pocket. The pocket where Horst Borsht's letter used to be.

# 16

Sam pointed himself north and walked unsteadily up the alley toward Beverly.

Everybody's entitled to a mistake now and again. Sam had more than made his quota for the day. He knew he was lucky to be alive. He could've been a hunk of meat back there — a tenant in one of those cold compartments Bumbera had warned him about. But the karate commando didn't want Sam dead. He just wanted the letter — and he'd got it. Well, maybe karate commando and company could figure out what Borsht meant and maybe not. Anyway, Sam had the damn thing memorized — so he still had a shot at it.

He made it to his building and walked up the back stairway. Sam couldn't help thinking of Nicky in the attic, eating oysters and screwing up courage for the big bamboosh with Mother. By the time he reached his office the ache in his head had quit doing somersaults and settled into one piercing arrow of pain directly between his ears.

"Gee," said Duchess, "back so soon? What happened with the man and the rocks?"

Sam ignored her and walked through his office and into the toilet that adjoined. He turned the cold water faucet on full blast and stuck his head under it. Then he took a hand towel and let it soak in the basin. He swallowed three aspirin.

Sam came back into his office, holding the hand towel on his head where it ached. Duchess stood there waiting for him.

"Look, Duchess, I don't feel so good. I'm gonna lie down for awhile." He started toward the black leather couch.

"You want me to tell him to wait — or come back later?"

"Tell who?"

"Mr. Gazelle."

Sam veered away from the couch and toward his swivel chair. "No, tell him to come in."

"Si-si."

It was a sort of subdued Mr. Zebra who was shown in by Duchess. Neither he nor Sam spoke until Duchess went out and closed the door. Part of what there was of her skirt got caught in the closing. She opened the door to free the material and closed it again.

"You just happen to be in the neighborhood?" Sam asked.

"Of course not — your call —"

"Yeah. You know anything about karate?"

"I beg your —"

"Stick out your hands. Both of them."

Mr. Zebra did, palms down.

"Turn 'em over." Sam put down the towel and took hold of Mr. Zebra's hands with both of his own. He let go almost immediately.

"No, it couldn't've been you. But then again, it could've been somebody working for you."

"I am completely in the dark —"

"So was I. OK — suppose I do a little listening while you do a little explaining."

"I am most grateful, Mr. Marlow, for your discretion earlier this morning."

"You're lucky. I usually can't wait to shoot off my mouth. What gives between you and the Beverly Hills brigade? You work for them?"

"Not exactly. I work for myself."

"Don't we all. Just what *is* your line of business?"

"I am a humble, reasonably corrupt opportunist."

"How'd you find out about the Eyes?"

"In prison. In Greece."

"You were in the same joint as Zinderneuf?"

"We were cellmates. You might say we were more than that."

"I never would've guessed."

"Zinderneuf and I were the only two civilized persons in the place. After a time he confided in me. Not completely, of course."

"Of course."

"He told me he had possession of the Eyes. I convinced him I could be of assistance in profitably disposing of them — very profitably. I would be out of prison sooner than he. I had contacts. I had often before negotiated the disposition of certain artifacts that couldn't be sold on the open market. Paintings, jewelry, other —"

"I get the picture."

"I made the necessary contacts with Mustafa Hakim and Alexander Anastas, whom I knew to be competitors as well as collectors. For this service I was to receive a 5 percent commission."

"So you're an agent. I should've known."

"Of course Zinderneuf never told me *where* the Eyes were hidden. But he wanted the bidding to take place here in Los Angeles. At first I wondered why. Then I found out. After I read the story of Borsht's murder in the paper Zinderneuf told me Borsht was his nephew. Zinderneuf also at that time admitted he did not have physical possession of the sapphires."

"And that's when you came to see me."

"Of course."

"You knew I'd been hired by the Borshts —

so you figured it was possible they had told me about the sapphires ol' Horst was holding for Uncle Wolfie."

"Yes."

"Well, it *is* possible. It's even possible he gave 'em to me for safekeeping before he died, or at least told me where they were hidden."

"Yes."

"Anything's possible. But what've you got to offer? Your twenty-five Gs is low bid. Hakim upped the pot to one hundred thousand."

"I am prepared to offer you half the profits."

Sam laughed. "You're offering me *half* of something I already have *all* of. What kind of agent talk is that?"

"I don't believe you presently have physical possession of the sapphires. You, Mr. Marlow, are a detective, and I am, as you say — an agent. If you obtain the sapphires and turn them over to me, I can promise you much more than one hundred thousand — much more."

"So you're double-crossing your old roomie, Zinderneuf?"

"I don't look at it that way."

"I guess your kind wouldn't. Would you consider this — a *third* for you?"

"And two-thirds for you?"

"No. A third for Borsht's daughter."

"You are a man of ethics, Mr. Marlow."

"Not necessarily."

"Yes. I would consider such a proposition."

"So would I," said Sam. "Now get out of here and let me get some sleep."

"Of course."

Mr. Zebra walked to the door.

"By the way," said Sam, "what were you in prison for?"

"Love. Someone was killed. An affair of the heart."

"Yeah," said Sam, "I hope he was worth it."


Sam slept. It was for more than a couple of hours. He woke when he heard the doorknob turn, the door open, and Duchess twitter. Standing behind Duchess, not twittering, was Elsa.

"I thought you'd be awake by now," said Duchess.

"Well, I wasn't," said Sam. "Elsa, what're you doing here? Anything happen?"

She shook her head. "My girl friend dropped me off. It's my turn to treat so I went to the fish store across the street and picked up some smoked salmon. If you'll drive me home we'll have dinner."

"Sure. I'm nuts about smoked salmon."

Sam would rather have had dinner with Gena, but that could come later. He had to do some talking to Elsa.

They got into the Plymouth and Sam turned the ignition key. He asked Elsa if her dad had ever told her about a couple of sapphires known as the Eyes of Alexander. She said no, and Sam believed her.

He told Elsa the story of the Eyes and Zinderneuf and her father. She was plainly astonished. He also told her that her father had obviously been afraid for his life and had left a message of some sort in code in that letter — the letter he no longer had. He had another lump on his head instead.

This time he parked the Plymouth directly in front of the house. As they walked up to the front door he had the feeling that something was wrong. He was right.

Elsa unlocked the door and they walked in. The parlor was a mess. The furniture had been slashed and torn apart — pictures ripped off the walls, drawers dumped, even the lamps smashed. The rest of the house was in the same shape — kitchen, bedrooms, even the bath and the half bath.

The window in the kitchen door was broken. That's how he, or they, had gotten in. Sam opened the door and looked out into the yard.

Three gunshots out of a silenced gun came as close as they could, splintering wood and glass around Sam's head. He ducked back into the kitchen and slammed the door shut. He pulled out the Luger and opened the door again just in time to see two men vault over the five-foot grape-trellis fence and disappear down the alley. Sam couldn't see their faces but one of the men was built just like Buster.

Sam walked into the garage and Elsa followed. The walls were lined with boxes about four feet wide and six feet high, with drawers and cabinets all painted green — and with the contents of the drawers and cabinets dumped all over the cement floor.

The contents consisted of just about everything imaginable — and all in doubles and triples. Necklaces, rings, guns, holsters, wallets, briefcases, clocks, knives, fountain pens, cigarette lighters, electric shavers, pocket watches, wrist watches, billy clubs, saps, boxing gloves, brass knuckles — but everything. All spattered and smashed to the floor — like an earthquake had hit.

"What the hell is all this?" Sam asked.

"Dad's prop boxes. Stuff he'd accumulated through the years. Even after he retired last year he still rented these things out to other prop men he knew."

Sam looked at the boxes. On them were decals, lettering, photographs — from studios, movies, and TV shows. Paramount, Columbia, Twentieth, Monogram, Allied Artists, Four Star, Ziv — *Murder by Moonlight, The Boss, The Islanders, The Rebel, Hondo, The Crimson Hawk, The Divers.*

"Well," said Sam, "we'd better call Bumbera. And I'd better figure out what to tell him and what not to. If Hacksaw ever finds out about that letter he'll probably shoot me in the back. You follow my lead."

Bumbera and Hacksaw were there in fifteen minutes. Sam was selective in what he said. He told them the history of the Eyes and how they ended up with Horst Borsht and that that's probably why Horst Borsht ended up dead. Sam mentioned Wolf Zinderneuf, Mustafa Hakim, Mr. Zebra, and even Alexander Anastas. They were all interested parties, all looking for the sapphires. Maybe one of them already had them. Ski Mask and the other gunman probably worked for one of them. Maybe they'd found the sapphires in Borsht's prop boxes — maybe they hadn't. The odds were they hadn't. That was about all there was to it, said Sam. And that was virtually true — except for the letter.

"OK, Sam. I'll look up some of these peo-

134

ple first thing in the morning — see if your story and theirs check out. You bought yourself a little more time."

"Yeah," said Hacksaw. "One of these days you're gonna buy some big trouble."

"Bummy, why don't you get yourself an organ grinder and him a tin cup? You'd have a great act."

"Why, you sonofabitch, I'll —" Hacksaw grabbed Sam by the shoulder and Sam hit him a left in the belly. Bumbera jumped between them.

"Cut it out! Both of you! Now, Hack, I'm gonna pull you off the case —"

"Pull him off the case? Hell, he wouldn't know a sapphire from a 7-Up. If I didn't tell him —"

"Shut up, Sam. Now I'm warning you. I've let you get away with some of this and some of that — for reasons of my own. But don't push. Not me or any other police officer, including Hack. Or I'll set your britches on fire. You hear me?"

"OK, OK, I hear you."

"Miss Borsht, I'll station a team of officers outside. You won't be bothered again."

"She's gonna spend the night at my secretary's place," said Sam. "She can't sleep in this mess."

"Good idea." Bumbera nodded. "But I'll

leave the team at the house anyhow in case —"

"No, Sam, I'm going to stay here."

Sam shrugged.

"The boys'll be outside. Come on, Hack. What a screwed-up situation."

"Hell," smiled Sam, "you think this is screwed up? You ever see a picture called *The Big Sleep*? 1946, Warner Brothers. You could sit through it eighty-eight times and still not know what the plot was. Faulkner, Leigh Brackett, and Jules Furthman wrote the script, and it's a cinch they never talked to each other. I think each one did every third page on his own and Howard Hawks just shot it and hoped for the best. Bogart and Bacall were great but I'll bet they didn't know what it was about either unless they read the book."

"Come on," said Hacksaw. "Let's get outa here."

Elsa fixed the salmon with thinly sliced on-ions and lemon. They had a couple of beers with it.

"Sam," she said, "my dad was a good man."

"Yeah, and he was a good soldier. They were all good soldiers. Just doing what they were ordered to do. And they were all good fathers and brothers and sons and nephews."

"What do you mean?"

"I don't know what I mean. It's tough to tell the enemy without a uniform. You know how to end all wars? Make everybody fight naked. Nobody would know who to kill and that would be the end of it."

"Sam —"

"No, I mean it. And let the women get in there naked too. That'd cinch it. No more war — just peace on earth and a lot of whoopee."

Sam could taste the salmon on her mouth when they kissed near the door. It wasn't just the salmon. She was built good, looked good, even smelled good. But somehow the sum didn't equal the parts. It was like that with certain women — and men too — oh hell, maybe he was just handing himself a line. Maybe Gena had just got him crazy. Maybe she had him fixed so no other woman in the world would be right. There'd always be something wrong. Maybe.

As he pulled away in his Plymouth Sam waved to the team of plainclothesmen parked in front of the house. They didn't wave back.

It was only 7:30 when he got home and called Gena.

"Would you like to go to a little party tonight?" she asked.

"I thought we were having one of our own."

"That comes later." Her voice was driving him nuts.

He could see her face, pure and plaintive the way she looked in *Never Let Me Go* when she was a Russian ballerina in love with Gable and Gable had to get her out from behind the Iron Curtain.

"What sort of a little party?"

"I'll surprise you."

"You already have."

"Sam! I'll pick you up in half an hour. Wear a dark suit."

"OK. Is a boutonniere required?"

"Only *you* are required."

# 17

Sam gargled, shaved, showered, and then brushed his teeth. He wanted to make sure he got rid of the salmon taste. He'd put on his best dark-blue suit and was gargling again when the doorbell rang three times.

"I knocked," she said. "Three times, but there was no answer."

"I was in the powder room. Come in a minute." She was done in white again — an evening dress, very décolleté. She didn't wear a brassiere, or need one. The white material was softer and filmier than the bedsheet last night but it had the same effect. It followed every sweep and bend of her sinuous body, outlining the nakedness beneath. On the right side of the gown a slit ran up her calf, past her knee, and about three inches into the thigh area. When she moved it did wonders for the gown — and vice versa.

She came into the room and Sam closed the door. She put her arms around him and kissed him. He was hooked and he knew it. But was that bad? Yes, it was, and he knew that too. He'd have to do something about it — later.

"Sam." She moved away. "You ought to save a little."

"Don't worry, I got plenty left."

"Yes, I know."

"What kind of a party is this?"

"Cocktail."

"Where?"

"On a boat. I'll drive."

She did. Sam was so busy looking at her face and her decolletage and the slit up her skirt that he didn't notice they were being tailed — again.

It was dark by the time they got to Newport, one of those velvety starless summer nights. She parked. They got out of the Ferrari and she led the way toward the pier and the "boat" that was docked there. As they walked Sam took the Luger out of his coat pocket and tucked it into the belt under his suit coat.

They arrived at the gangplank that linked the pier to the ship. A name was painted on the hull: *Eurydice.* A fellow in uniform stood on the pier; another one just like him stood aboard ship on the other side of the gangplank.

"Evening, Miss Anastas. Good evening, sir," the first uniformed fellow said.

"Evening, Jimmy," she replied.

"It's not as big as a battleship," Sam said.

"Actually it's a converted minesweeper." Gena smiled.

"Yeah? Who converted it?"

"My father."

"What's a Eurydice?"

"That was my mother's name."

"Good evening, Miss Anastas," the other uniformed fellow said. "Good evening, sir. The others have all arrived. They're in the saloon."

"Thank you, Timmy," Gena said.

"Talking bookends," Sam remarked.

"Twins." Gena smiled.

It was old home week in the saloon. The joint was glutted with familiar if not friendly faces, starting with paterfamilias himself — Commodore Alexander Anastas looked even bigger aboard ship than he did in Holmby Hills. Teresa Anastas was dressed in red, wearing a half bra that pushed her breasts up almost to her shoulders so they looked like a couple of salad bowls of shimmering Jello. And every man there except the Commodore was watching Teresa's breasts shimmering as she walked across the room. The men included Mustafa Hakim — in a blue tuxedo, blue shirt, blue bow tie, and even very dark blue patent leather shoes — Wolf Zinderneuf, Mr. Zebra, and George, all in basic black tuxedos. George was doing his furtive best not to look at Teresa but he just couldn't keep his eyes off her bobbing baubles.

Cynthia Ashley looked perfect in a powder-blue two-piece evening dress — the personification of feminine dignity as she sipped her martini and chatted politely with her hulking host.

A four-piece orchestra played appropriate background music and two uniformed men and a woman moved around proffering hors d'oeuvres and drinks. The hors d'oeuvres included caviar, terrapin, crab, shrimp, and some exotic concoctions Sam couldn't label. But he could label the booze, all right — nothing but the best. Sam ordered a gin and tonic. So did Gena.

"Ah, Mr. Marlow — we meet again." Anastas came over and shook hands with Sam. The hand was about as big as a boxing glove and hard as mahogany. Sam couldn't help thinking of those hands all over Teresa's breasts.

"Yeah," said Sam. "Small world, big business."

"Enjoy yourself, sir. And I *would* like to speak with you later if you have a moment."

"I'm all ears — and eyes," Sam remarked, hitting the "eyes" a little harder.

The Commodore grunted and moved away.

"Come on," Sam said to Gena. "I'll introduce you to some of these people."

He did. Mustafa Hakim held her hand a moment too long. Zinderneuf clicked off one of his sharpest clicks and Mr. Zebra, reeking of lavender, kissed Gena's hand with his courtliest continental coxcombry.

The meeting between Gena Anastas and Cynthia Ashley was something to see. They both reeked of civility, but underneath the surface they were looking at each other like a couple of Siamese cats sizing up the opposition before an alley fight. They purred politely and were *so* happy to know each other. If it ever happened, that would be an alley fight worth watching — tooth and claw and protect the jugular in the clinches.

After a little more purring Gena eased Sam away from Cynthia and toward Teresa. "Teresa, you look lovely tonight," Gena said. "That gown's new, isn't it?"

"Yes." Teresa smiled. "Your father selected it."

The old boy's not blind yet, Sam thought to himself, trying not to stare at Mrs. Anastas' bulbous breastworks.

"Teresa." It was the Commodore's voice, from across the saloon. "Would you come here, please?"

"Excuse me." Teresa smiled again and

walked toward Anastas, who was talking with his erstwhile partner Mustafa Hakim.

"Swell party," Sam said, "but I think they'd all like to poison each other."

"You think that of me too, Sam?"

"No. You and I are the good guys. We wouldn't use poison."

"But isn't that the way it is?" she said. "In business? In politics? In life? People pretending one thing and meaning another?"

"Yeah, Angel. That's the way it is."

"But not between us, Sam. Let's never pretend with each other. Promise?"

"Cross my heart and hope to die."

It was almost an hour later when the Commodore got his moment with Sam. "Sir, it seems fate has brought us together."

"Fate — and your daughter."

"Quite right. And quite a coincidence."

"Stranger things have happened — and probably will again."

"I told you my passion is collecting."

"I'd say you've done OK. You've collected everything in the world except a little loose change."

"Not quite, sir. But I intend to have them. I must have them — hold them in these hands and see them with these eyes, while there's still time. I *must*."

"I gotcha."

"Whatever Hakim has bid, I will better."

"The pot's up to one hundred thousand."

"One hundred twenty-five."

"Just like that?"

"Yes."

"I count three men dead in the last forty-eight hours. Two of 'em I killed myself. That ought to be worth one-fifty."

"Agreed."

"Not that fast. 'Cause if I find out you hired those gunsels . . ."

"I give you my word, sir."

"And I take your word, Commodore — for now. And I'll think about your offer."

Mustafa Hakim walked over and extended his hand to Anastas. "Thank you for your hospitality, Commodore. I'd like you to see *my* yacht some time."

"Leaving so early?" the Commodore asked. By now both Gena and Cynthia had joined them.

"Yes," said Hakim. "I'm giving a little party of my own this evening. Mr. Marlow, perhaps you and Miss Anastas would care to join us. I've taken over the Blue Fez — it's a cafe on —"

"Yeah, I know the place."

"Please, do come." Hakim looked at Gena. "I think you'll find it amusing."

Good nights flew thick and fast all over the

place and in five minutes Sam, Gena, George, Mrs. Anastas, and the Commodore were the only ones left besides the hired help.

George said his good night and walked toward the door.

"Watch your head, Georgie," Sam said. George made no acknowledgment.

"You won't forget our little chat, will you, sir?" the Commodore asked Sam.

"Never in a million years," Sam replied. "Mrs. Anastas, you're a great hostess. Someday they ought to name a boat after you."

"Good night, Teresa," Gena said quickly, as if she were trying to erase Sam's remark from the record. "Good night, Commodore." She ushered Sam out onto the deck.

"It's a nice night for love," said Sam as he looked around the deck.

"That wasn't a very nice thing you said in there."

"Wasn't it?"

"No — and you know it." She kissed him.

"That kind of thing can do wonders for my manners."

"Come on," she said.

More good nights from Timmy and Jimmy, and then Sam and Gena were on the pier walking toward the parking lot.

"How'd you like to come on my boat sometime?" she asked.

"Is it as big as the Commodore's?"

"No, but it's big enough."

"Then why don't we take a trip to China?" Sam said.

"Fine."

"What do you call your boat?"

"*Veltio Avrio.*"

"Yeah? What does that mean?"

That's when the torpedo stepped from behind a post and put the gun right in Sam's face. At the same time another man moved from another post and covered Gena's mouth with his hand. The second man had his jaw wired.

"Hello, Ralph," Sam said, "how's everything at Cane's Club?"

"Better than your face is gonna be, smart guy. I'm gonna work you over."

"Yeah? Is Jock gonna work her over?"

"She's gonna watch you get it, you smartass. Sucker punchin' — breakin' people's jaws —"

Sam made a noise like he was clearing his throat. He was. He spat an oyster right into Ralph's left eye, knocked the gun away, and smashed Ralph's nose with a straight right shot. The nose erupted geysers of blood all over Ralph's face. Another fast left-right combination sent Ralph senseless against a parked car. In an instant Sam turned toward Gena and Jock. Gena stamped her heel on Jock's foot. He let her go and as Sam charged toward him Jock covered his face with both hands. "No," he said, "not in the face, please." He didn't say it very plainly because the wiring in his jaw had broken loose again.

Sam gut-hit him with a left and a right, twisted him around, and kicked him off the dock and into the water below. Jock made a big splash. Sam walked over to Ralph, picked up the gun, and dragged the still senseless torpedo to the edge of the dock. Sam threw him into the water, then tossed the gun after him. Two splashes — one big, one little.

Sam walked back to Gena. "What did you say the name of your boat was?"

"*Veltio Avrio.*"

"What does that mean?"

"It's Greek for 'Better Tomorrow.' "

"That's very — optimistic."

"Sam," she said. "I don't think there's ever been anyone quite like you."

"Not quite," Sam agreed.

# 18

As she drove Sam cracked the knuckles of both his hands. Gena stopped the Ferrari for a red light.

"Do your hands hurt?" she asked.

"Some."

"Let me kiss them and make them better."

She did.

"It hurts here, too." Sam touched his lips with a fingertip. "And other places." But the light turned green. Gena smiled and gunned the Ferrari.

"Sam," she frowned, "I'm afraid Petey Cane will make more trouble. He may still have other prints of those pictures . . ."

"No, Angel, I don't think Cane had anything to do with that visit back there. I think those two boys were just sitting around drinking too much brave-maker and convincing themselves how tough they were. They both reeked of booze. Well, anyhow, they got the whole Pacific Ocean for a chaser."

"You were wonderful."

"I just didn't like that mug putting his paws on you."

"Please, let's change the subject."

"All right. Say, you ever see a picture called *Lady in the Lake?* MGM, 1947. Robert Montgomery played a private eye. But you never saw his face in the picture unless he was looking into a mirror. It was all shot from his point of view — pretty interesting. Trouble is, the human eye has a lot wider peripheral vision than a camera lens. You always felt cheated. But not by Audrey Totter — she was good in it. Montgomery and Totter made another picture together called *The Saxon Charm* . . ."

"Sam — do you know everything about movies?"

"Nobody knows everything about anything."

"But you must've seen an awful lot of them."

"Sure. Don't you know that movies are your best entertainment? Well, almost — except for . . ."

"Now, Sam."

"Speaking of entertainment — your place or mine?"

"Don't you want to go to Mr. Hakim's party?"

"I could live without it."

"He said it would be amusing."

"Mr. Hakim is about as amusing as a snakebite."

"Oh." She smiled. "Let's just stop in for a few minutes."

"Sure. Just let me know when you've had enough."

The Blue Fez was on one of the seedier sections of Sunset Boulevard. Sam had often driven by but had never had occasion to stop in. He wasn't so sure of this occasion either, but what the hell — maybe Hakim would up the ante or maybe Sam would find out who had the letter or maybe anything.

Sam knocked on the locked door. After a couple of beats it was opened by a dusky mastodon who stood about seven feet tall, weighed three hundred pounds, wore nothing but baggy silk pants and a turban — and carried a wicked-looking curved sword about five feet long.

"Hakim sent us," said Sam.

The mastodon bowed from his bulging belly and motioned for Gena and Sam to come inside.

"Where's the lamp that goes with you?" Sam asked him.

No reply. The giant led them through the dark empty main room toward a door, and music that sounded right out of Port Said. The giant opened the door. The three of them went in to face the music.

The room hung heavy with vapors of smoke

151

— and not from ordinary American cigarettes, or even ordinary Turkish tobacco. Hashish. About a dozen people sat on pillows on the floor in a wide semicircle, with food and booze and Turkish pipes all over the place. It looked like a scene from one of the Maria Montez-Jon Hall pictures Universal-International used to make in the '40s.

The pillow people included Mustafa Hakim, cross-legged in the center of the semicircle, his executive secretary Cynthia Ashley next to him. Wolf Zinderneuf, Mr. Zebra, and — just to show how democratic the blue man was feeling — even Turhan the skinny sat with them. The rest were a mixed bag — men and women, blacks, orientals, and some of indeterminate origin.

Half a dozen beautiful, nearly naked girls on loan from some caliph's harem were dishing out shish kebab, goat, stuffed grape leaves, and flat, round Syrian bread, and pouring anisette all over the place.

Mustafa Hakim rose to greet them. "Delighted to see you both," he said. His pupils were dilated and he had a silly smirk on his bluish face. "Come sit next to me."

What he meant was for Gena to sit next to him and he managed it smoothly, signaling Cynthia to move down the line. There was that look between the two Siamese cats again.

"Would you care for anisette?" he asked Gena.

"Thank you," she said.

"I thought liquor and tobacco never touched your lips," Sam said.

"Only on special occasions." His dilated pupils were looking right at Gena. The slimy bastard, Sam thought to himself.

"To special occasions!" Hakim toasted.

"Confusion to the enemy," said Sam and drank some of the sweet stuff.

Mustafa Hakim looked in the direction of the four fezzed musicians and nodded. Immediately the tempo of the music changed to a more throbbing, pulsating beat. Hakim touched Gena's forearm with the tips of his fingers and leaned his head toward her. With his free hand he indicated the musical instruments: "Derberki — bouzouki — oud — and kanoon."

"Yeah," said Sam. "My lawyers are Ogalvie, Ogalvie, Dietz, and Schwartz."

"Unfortunately," Hakim continued, "the art of belly dancing is unappreciated outside the Orient. But it is an art form that dates back nearly four thousand years. It is the most sensual and sexually exciting of all dances when properly performed. But it is becoming more difficult to find —"

"Is this a long story?" Sam said loudly.

Hakim clapped three times. "No further words are necessary." The music got even wilder and from behind a curtain at the side of the room came three of the shapeliest, most beautiful brunettes this side of the Tigris and Euphrates, twisting and winding their way toward the semicircle.

The brunettes were wearing castanets on their fingers and not much else anyplace else. All three were big girls, full-bosomed and full-hipped, with supple, rippling bellies. Some of the musicians commenced to sing — it sounded more like wailing — as if they were urging the dancers on.

The dancers didn't need urging. They were trying to outdo each other with gyrating, heaving bodies, slithering around and about. Their melonlike breasts were rolling and shaking, superb hips weaving, groins quivering to the castanets, long snaking arms always moving from their curving, dipping shoulders.

Hakim and his entourage clapped and chanted and reached out toward the majestically moving legs of the dancers as they swirled and thrust their bellies in lasso-like patterns. Sam and Gena were the only two not chanting and clapping. Even Zinderneuf was beating his wooden hand on the floor in time to the throbbing, frenzied music. And all but Sam and Gena were swaying their shoulders and heads to the exotic tempo.

Then the dancers concentrated more and more on their host, plunging their vibrating bellies and buttocks closer and closer to Mustafa Hakim — who sipped his anisette and smiled wide-eyed at the oscillating brunettes.

Then Hakim motioned to Cynthia Ashley. She rose, walked over, and bent near him. He whispered something. She looked at the dancers. He whispered again. It seemed as if she started to shake her head but didn't. Hakim stared at her until she rose again and walked into the semicircle with the coiling, twisting belly dancers.

Cynthia Ashley's face was a death mask, as if she were trying to transport her body and sensibilities to some other place. She looked at Hakim again. It was more than a look — it was a supplication, maybe a prayer. Whatever it was, it went unanswered. And in the next moment Cynthia Ashley's perfection peeled off her like the skin of a snake.

Slowly, awkwardly, uncertainly, she tried to move her untrained body to the pulsating rhythm of the music. The three belly dancers swirled around her, swishing their hips and bellies, their long, curling black hair fluttering and tumbling around their shoulders.

She tried. She did that. Cynthia Ashley writhed her firm Occidental hips; she moved her arms and made rotating motions with her ascending breasts. She moved long, gown-hobbled legs as best she could, looking at no one but Mustafa Hakim and waiting for a sign from him saying she could stop — that the joke had gone far enough. But it hadn't.

As she continued her tormented motions, trying to move with the belly dancers, Hakim made a different sign. He slowly moved both his hands to the center of his chest, then away. It seemed she would surely lose control and run — the others, seated on either side of Hakim, clapped and laughed and chanted in anticipation of what was to come. All but Gena and Sam.

Still moving on the dance floor, Cynthia Ashley unbuttoned the blouse of her evening gown. She slipped the powder-blue blouse off her shoulders, revealing a see-through flesh-colored brassiere, then let the blouse drop to the floor. The audience clapped even harder and laughed and yelled.

At first Cynthia tried to dance so her back was mostly to the semicircle, but then she was exposed to the musicians — so she had to keep moving and dancing, still trying to avoid the eyes of Mustafa Hakim in fear of what he might order next. But she couldn't avoid his eyes. Hakim made another motion — and the exhortation from his guests peaked to a crazy, discordant, obscene crescendo.

The three brunette belly dancers fanned farther away from Cynthia and finally stood still with their feet and legs apart. Their shoulders, breasts, bellies, and buttocks moved in suggestive sweeps and grinds.

Cynthia Ashley unbuttoned the long tight skirt and let it fall from her hips and down her long slender legs to her feet. She wore only the briefest of flesh-colored panties, fringed with a rim of fine blue lace.

She stepped away from the spilled skirt and danced. A few moments ago Cynthia Ashley had looked the essence of sophistication and elegance — cultured voice and graceful movements, dignified, almost unapproachable. Now she danced nearly naked — a crass, pathetic creature — exposing her flesh, her body, submitting like any prostitute — bending to the capricious whims and feeding the perverted appetites of Mustafa Hakim and his friends.

Sam looked at Gena. Her head was lowered toward the floor just in front of her.

Hakim's dreamy, languid eyes looked with dull amusement at his pathetic plaything dancing obscenely before him. Of course, he had seen her naked many times. That was part of the setup. And of course she had catered to his opprobrious perversions in private. That was part of the setup too. Sam could tell that this was her first public abasement. He couldn't tell how much further it would go. Mr. Zebra drooled with delight — then said something to Mustafa Hakim. Hakim smiled even more widely and nodded.

Gena's hand touched Sam's arm. "Sam."

"He said it would be amusing. Let me know when you've had enough."

"Please, let's get out of here."

Sam rose and helped Gena to her feet. The smell of the hashish, the primitive beat of the music, and the blond bogus belly dancer silhouetted in and out of the curling smoke conspired to make the room a miniature of Dante's *Inferno*.

Hakim looked up at Gena. "Don't go. The show is just starting."

"The first act was enough," said Sam. He led Gena away toward the door. But the door was closed, and at a motion from Hakim the giant with the five-foot sword stepped in front of it — and them.

Sam stopped, smiled at the giant, and started to turn back toward Hakim. Instead he kneed the giant directly in the groin and with a complementing motion hammered a straight left into his chest and a right cross to his jaw. The giant dropped like a shot buffalo. Sam took the fallen sword by the hilt and hurled it point-first toward the ceiling. It stuck there and quivered.

As he opened the door for Gena, Sam looked up at the sword. "Tyrone Power did that in *The Mark of Zorro*," he said.

Gena drove the Ferrari west on Sunset to Gower, south on Gower to Melrose, west on Melrose to Larchmont, and south on Larchmont. She made a U-turn in front of Sam's apartment house and switched off the ignition. Neither she nor Sam had spoken since they left the Blue Fez.

"Sam, why are people so cruel?"

"Different people — different reasons."

"That poor girl . . ."

"I didn't think you liked her."

"I felt so sorry for her. I've never seen anyone so humiliated — degraded."

"Haven't you?"

"You could have stopped it."

"Maybe I could've. I would've tried if she had made one move to get out of there. But she didn't."

"I despise him."

"Hakim? He's just one of the sharks in the

sea. Are we going upstairs?"

"Sam, the Commodore told me about the Eyes of Alexander. That's what everybody wants, isn't it?"

"That's not what I want."

"Whose side are you on?"

"Yours, Angel. If it's possible."

"Sam, I love you. But please, not tonight. After all that's happened, I've got to think things out."

"I love you too, Angel."

She kissed him tenderly. Then he got out of the car and leaned back in, holding the door open.

"*Veltio avrio* — maybe tomorrow'll be better," he said.

She nodded. "Thank you, Sam. Good night."

He closed the door and watched while she started the engine and pulled away.

Sam lay in bed in the dark. He had taken a heavy slug of the Grand Marnier and could still taste the orange brandy — and Gena Anastas, from the night before. He knew she hadn't been completely on the level with him. He tried to convince himself it wasn't Gena he was nuts about — it was the Gene Tierney of *Sundown, Laura, Leave Her to Heaven, On the Riviera, The Razor's Edge.*

160

The hell it was — it was Gena, damn it — it was Gena.

He slept. He dreamed of Gena. She was naked — doing a belly dance.

# 19

The next morning Sam drove to the Borsht house to check on things. A different team of cops was parked out front. Sam went over to talk to them. They both stared at the familiar figure leaning into the car window.

"The Lieutenant told us you looked like him, but Christ Almighty, it's like seeing a ghost," one of the cops said.

"Anything happen?" Sam asked.

"Nothing," the cop answered, "except for the other girl."

"What other girl?"

"Miss Borsht said she was a friend of hers."

Sam walked to the door quickly and knocked. The other girl opened the door and did a double take.

"You *do* look like Bogart!"

"Where's Elsa?" Sam stepped inside.

"Right here." Elsa was on the other side of the room straightening things out. "Sam, this is a friend of mine, Mona Davis — she's going to give me a hand today. I'm not going in to work."

"Oh," said Sam. "Glad to meet you, Mona."

"Want some coffee?" Elsa asked. "It's instant but it's good."

"No, thanks. Look Elsa, I've been thinking — are you *sure* about what your father said before he — when he saw you?"

"Not really sure. But it sounded like 'ein Schlag' — a hit or blow. My German's not too good."

"He didn't know me — or whose side I was on. I still think he was trying to tell you something. Maybe something that had to do with the letter. How do you say letter in German?"

"Uh, let me see. It's — I remember — 'Brief.' Yes, that's it — 'Brief.' "

"What's all this about?" Mona asked. "Can I be of help?"

"No, thanks." Sam pulled a card out of his pocket. "Elsa, write down what your father said."

Elsa did. "I'm not positive about the spelling but that ought to be pretty close."

"OK, thanks. Don't go anyplace without letting me know first."

As Sam was going out the door he heard Mona Davis say, "Gee, I wonder if they can fix me up to look like Raquel Welch!"

Sam drove to Larchmont and Beverly,

163

parked the Plymouth at the gas station, walked across the street, and headed toward his office. But that wasn't where he was going. He had an idea. He walked past the blind newsman, nodded to the "Hello, Sam," crossed to the east side of Larchmont, and walked rapidly to Chevalier's Book Store.

In the 1940s Mr. Chevalier would've been played by Miles Mander. He was of medium height, slightly bent forward as a lot of book-ish men are — handsome, with wavy white hair and a soothing, refined voice. Sam had become friendly with Chevalier in the past month. Until the last few days the detective business had been lousy so Sam had spent quite a bit of time going through books about movies and talking to Chevalier about rare and out-of-print editions on the motion picture business.

Sam said hello to Madeline and Pat, who worked in the store, as he walked to the desk. Mr. Chevalier was there, slightly bent over a book.

"Howdy," said Sam.

"Good morning." Mr. Chevalier unhooked the half-glasses from his ears and removed them from his aquiline nose. "You haven't been in for a few days, Sam. I ran across a book I think —"

"I appreciate that, Mr. Chevalier, but right

now maybe you can help me with something else."

"My pleasure."

Sam pulled the card out of his pocket. "Have you got a German dictionary around here?"

"Yes, certainly. But I do speak German quite fluently, you know."

"You do?"

"And French, Italian, also —"

"Just German'll do fine. What do you make outa this?"

Chevalier took the card and hooked the half-glasses back over his ears and nose.

"Ein Schlag — a hit, a blow."

"That much I got. Could it mean anything else? Something to do with a letter?"

"Letter would be 'Brief.' "

"Check. Look maybe there's another word that sounds like it. See, this was *said,* not *written,* so it could've sounded like mein Schlag or dumm Schlag — or groomschalla —"

"Enough!!" Mr. Chevalier unhooked his glasses again. "As Holmes would say, 'elementary.' "

"What is, for Chrissake?"

"You say it may have something to do with a letter?"

"Maybe."

"Do you have the letter on you?"

"No, but I've got it memorized. It goes like this — 'under the tramp of mar—' "

"Do you have the envelope?"

"The what?"

"The envelope. 'Umschlag' in German means envelope. In northern Germany the —"

"The envelope! Where the hell is it?" Sam shouted. "I put the letter in my pocket, but what the hell did I do with the — it's on the desk! It's on my desk in the office!" He turned and started to run out of the store past Madeline and Pat.

"Thanks!" he hollered back. "Thanks — *Umschlag! Umschlag!*"

Sam jayran across the street and raced up Larchmont Boulevard to his building, took the steps three at a time, and was in Duchess's office in thirty seconds.

"Hi!" Duchess said.

Sam ran past her and into his office. Duchess followed him.

"Whatsamatter, Sam? What's the hurry?"

He pointed to the rolltop. "It's not here!"

"What's not?"

"The Umschlag! The damned envelope!"

"Yeah! Don't the place look neat? I cleaned things up."

"Duchess, what did you do with the envelope?"

166

"Threw it in the wastebasket with the other stuff."

Sam rushed to the wastebasket. "It's empty!"

"Yeah, I cleaned that out afterwards."

"Duchess, where did you throw the stuff from the wastebasket?"

"Downstairs in the bin in the alley."

"When?"

"Last night."

"You come with me." Sam ran out of the office, down the hall, and down the back stairway with Duchess trying to keep up with him.

"Jeesus, Sam, what're you so excited about?"

"Duchess, you haven't thrown anything out since you came to work for me — why last night?"

"I don't know — the banana peels were piling up and — I don't know — I just cleaned up. *Sam!*"

Duchess's heel hooked about halfway down the stairs and she started to fall. Sam turned and caught her in his arms.

"Now look!" She was nearly crying. "I broke a heel."

"The hell with the heel, come on."

Sam ran out the back door and around the corner of the building to the bin in the alley with Duchess limping along after him on one high heel and one no heel.

"It's empty! The damn bin's empty!"

"Are you sure?" Duchess scuttled up alongside him.

"Am I *sure?* Duchess, for God's sake, can't you see, the damn thing's empty!"

"You're right," she nodded. "It *is* empty."

Mr. Sing, the gentleman who ran the Chinese laundry behind the doughnut shop, came out the back door carrying a cardboard box filled with stuff to be thrown out. On Mr. Sing's left shoulder there perched a parrot.

"Mr. Sing," said Sam.

"Hello!" said the parrot.

"Hello," said Sam to the parrot. "Mr Sing —"

"Mr. Bogart," said Mr. Sing.

"Marlow," said Sam.

"Hello," said the parrot.

"Hello," said Sam. "Look, Mr. Sing — did you see the garbage truck come by this morning?"

"Yes, Mr. Bogart."

"Marlow," said Sam. "How long ago?"

"Hour ago," said Mr. Sing.

"Hello," said the parrot.

"What's the name of the company that picks up the garbage here?" Sam asked.

"Western. Western Disposal," said Mr. Sing.

"Hello!" said the parrot.

"Goodbye," said Sam. "Come on, Duchess. Thanks, Mr. Sing."

"You're welcome, Mr. Bogart."

"Hello," said the parrot.

Sam got the number of Western Disposal from the operator, called, and asked to talk to the boss. The boss's name was Louie Saakalian. Louie sounded exactly like Akim Tamiroff over the phone.

Sam explained that he had to get something back that had been picked up this morning from this address. He asked where the Western Disposal truck would take the stuff.

"The dump," Louie said.

"Which dump?"

"Mission Canyon Road Dump off Sepulveda. Truck should be there pretty quick."

"What's the number of the truck?"

"Number seven. My boy Dominick driving. Number seven. You won't find it."

"What?" asked Sam. "The truck?"

"No, what you're looking for. You won't find it."

"Thanks, Louie," said Sam, and slammed the phone into the cradle. "Come on, Duchess."

"Where we going, Sam?"

"To see if we can beat number seven to the dump."

# 20

Sam just about ripped the gears off the Plymouth getting there — but he didn't beat ol' number seven of Western Disposal. It was one of three empty garbage trucks on its way out of the Mission Canyon Road Dump.

Sam pulled up on the driver's side of number seven and waved it to a stop. "Dominick! Hey, Dominick!"

"Holy Christ!" said Dominick to the fellow next to him. "This guy's a dead ringer for Bogart." Dominick turned back to Sam. "How do you know my name?"

"Your dad and I went to school together."

"In Armenia?"

"Yeah. Where did you dump the load?"

"Right over there where that cat's working." Dominick pointed toward a tractor pushing and leveling refuse.

"Thanks, Dom!" Sam shifted gears and gunned the Plymouth. About forty yards farther on he drove off the road and over the garden of garbage to the spot Dominick had indicated.

"Come on Duchess — out."

"Sam, I only got one heel."

"Find the envelope and I'll buy you ten pairs of shoes."

They got out of the car and onto the garbage.

"Jeeze, it stinks!" said Duchess, holding her nose.

"Look for stuff from the doughnut shop. That'll mean we're getting close." Sam plunged both hands into the garbage. He scooped out eggshells, onion peelings, coffee grounds, bottle caps, fish heads, cigar butts, TV dinner plates, tin cans, a truss and diverse odorous objects of uncertain specification.

Duchess limped and weaved along the refuse, gingerly poking with one hand and still pinching her nose with the other.

"Use both hands, Duchess — this is no time to be finicky!" Sam hollered.

The tractor swept closer to where Sam and Duchess waded in the waste of Western Disposal. "Hey!" the driver yelled, "get the hell out of there before you get plowed under!"

"Take it easy, friend," Sam yelled back.

"I'm telling you —" Now the driver was close enough to observe and appreciate Duchess's long-legged, short-skirted body. He was fascinated by the sight of this beautiful curvaceous blond limping and bending and dipping. She pitched and fell, her fluttering little skirt well above her thighs, and he stood up for a better view. Sam went over to help Duchess to her feet. Still standing, the driver yelled, "What the hell are you doing?"

"Pearl diving," Sam yelled back.

"Get outa there! I'm coming through!"

"Take a detour!" Sam spotted something and stooped to pick it up. "Duchess, look!"

"What is it?" Duchess wiped at her chin with her forearm.

"Half a doughnut! Our stuff's got to be right around here!"

The driver cursed and slammed his cap on the floorboard of the tractor. "I'm coming through — get your asses outa there!" He sat, geared up the tractor, and started toward them. Sam pulled the Luger out of his pocket and pointed it at the oncoming cat. That did it. The driver turned a hard right and kept on going away from them, plowing a path of garbage as he went. Sam plunged the Luger into his pocket and cried out.

"Look, Duchess!"

"The envelope?"

"Banana peels! It's got to be right around here!"

It was — soiled and wrinkled, but there it was. Sam picked it up and kissed the Umschlag.

"Now that we got it, what're we gonna do

172

with it?" Duchess wanted to know.

" 'Under the tramp of marching feet,' " Sam recited, " 'under the beat of daring drum. Follow the three beneath the post.' — Age. . . . That's *it!*"

"Hell, Sam," Duchess said, "I don't know what you're talking about — all I know is I smell like —"

"Look at the stamp — the postage stamp!"

On the stamp was a picture of three Revolutionary War soldiers marching with fife and drum and flag. "The answer to the riddle is right under the postage stamp. All we've got to do is steam it off." Sam hugged Duchess and kissed her on the forehead.

"Terrific," she said, "but first could we take a shower?"

# 21

In his apartment Sam had showered and changed clothes. Duchess had showered, washed her drip-dry dress, and hung it up. She walked into the kitchen wearing one of Sam's shirts. He had carefully steamed the stamp off the envelope and was smiling.

"There it is. The Dutchman gave good directions. All we got to do is go and pick them up."

"Sam, do you mind if I pass? I'm just not up to it."

"That's OK, Duchess. You don't need to go."

"Go where?"

"First I've got to call Elsa. She ought to be in on it. I guess they belong to her."

"What belongs to her? Sam, you don't need a secretary — you need an interpreter."

Sam winked, put the envelope in his pocket, went to the phone, and called Elsa. But Elsa didn't answer. Mona Davis did.

"What do you mean she's not there?" Sam asked. "Where is she?"

"Well, you ought to know," Mona said.

"You're the one who called her. She went to meet you."

Sam had a sinking feeling. "Did the cops go with her?"

"No, they're still out front. I saw Elsa talking to them but they're still here."

"How long ago?"

"Not too long after you left."

Sam hung up. "Damn!" he said and twitched.

"What's happened now?" Duchess asked. Sam ignored the question and dialed Bumbera. He was there but he seemed in a hurry.

"Look, Bummy, I think you better get out an APB on Elsa Borsht. I'm afraid —"

"So am I," Bumbera interrupted. "We just got a report. Couple of kids found a girl's body in one of the caves up at Bronson Canyon . . ."

"Any ID?" Sam snapped.

"No, she was naked. But the description fits. I was just going up there."

"I'll meet you —"

"You know where it is?"

"Yeah."

Sam went to the closet, pulled out the spare trench coat, slipped it on, and put the Luger in his pocket.

"Duchess, when your dress is dry call a cab."

"But Sam —"

The door slammed.

Bronson Canyon is less than ten minutes from Hollywood and Vine toward Los Feliz and north of Franklin Avenue — a rock-blanketed stretch rimmed by craggy cliffs on three sides. With the exception of the sound stages and back lots, more movies and television episodes have been shot in Bronson Canyon than anyplace else in Hollywood. From *I Am a Fugitive from a Chain Gang* with Muni to *The Searchers* with the Duke, *Ride the High Country* with Joel McCrea and Randolph Scott — plus just about every TV western, including *Wyatt Earp*, *Bonanza*, *The Deputy*, *Gunsmoke*, *The Rebel*, *Lawman*, *The Virginian*. Everything and anything with horses and guns, cowboys and Indians: more gunshots were fired in Bronson Canyon than at Gettysburg. More movie good guys and bad guys died there than anyplace else on earth.

As Sam drove into the rugged Griffith Park area he knew somebody up there was really dead — not with blanks and blood capsules, not movie dead where they could get up and die again if it didn't look good for the camera — but dead dead, where there were no "take two's." Sam knew it was somebody. He just hoped to Christ it wasn't Elsa.

The Plymouth laid a wake of dust up the

dirt road and topped out on the barren rock-walled canyon.

There were a couple of cop cars at the entrance to one of the caves on the right. Hacksaw, a few other cops, and two kids — maybe ten or twelve years old, with blanched faces — were standing at the entrance. Sam parked and walked past them without saying a word. Hacksaw followed him.

Bumbera and a couple more cops were inside. He or somebody had draped a blanket over the body.

"I'm sorry, Sam," Bumbera said.

That's all he needed to say. That said it all. Sam wiped a hand over his face and knelt by the blanket. His hand trembled; it was cold and sweaty. He lifted a corner of the blanket.

Sam had only known her a few days. He had met a lot of people in those few days — but of all of them Sam felt that Elsa Borsht was the only one who had been completely honest with him. She wasn't the brightest, the strongest, the most beautiful. But she was the most honest. She trusted him — and now she was a corpse.

The lips where he had kissed her were split and swollen. Two, maybe more, teeth were knocked out. There were bruises on her cheek and around one of her eyes. And Sam couldn't keep his eyes completely dry.

"They beat her to death?"

Bumbera shook his head. "Don't think so. Take a look at her left arm."

Sam pulled the blanket down, accidentally exposing her breasts. He covered her quickly except for the left arm. There were needle marks not very carefully made.

"They pumped her full of something," Bumbera said. "Probably to make her talk when the working over didn't do it."

"OK," said Sam.

"She was your first client, wasn't she?" Hacksaw asked.

Sam sprang at the sergeant like a panther, but Bumbera grabbed him and so did a couple of other cops.

"I'll kill that sonofabitch!" Sam growled.

"Not today you won't — or any other day!" Bumbera said. "Now get a hold on yourself."

Sam breathed deeply, nodded and pulled himself free.

"Yeah, Hacksaw." Sam nodded again. He was still shaking. "I guess you could say she was my first client. And I told her to stay in that house. The house those cops of yours are still guarding while this kid's up here dead."

"Sam," Bumbera said softly, "take it easy. Nobody's to blame. Not you or us. They tricked her out of there — and she got it. It happens."

"It happens to the wrong people. She was the only decent —"

"OK, Sam, you can torture yourself crazy. But not if you're gonna stay in the detective business."

"Oh, I'm gonna stay in the business, all right. And somebody's gonna be *out* of business."

"The dumbest thing you can do, Sam, is to get mad. That's the way to get killed."

"Bummy, I'm not mad — just mean. Now will you do me a favor — a big one? I'll owe you."

"What?"

"You've got an unidentified body here. Keep it that way until tomorrow."

"Sam, I can't —"

"Sure you can, Bummy — just till I call you tomorrow."

Bumbera shook his head. "You ask too much."

"No I don't. Just enough — and you know it."

"The reporters . . ."

"They don't have to see her face — not if you don't let them. Please, Bummy. I'm not cracking wise now. I'm begging you."

"OK, OK. You heard it, Hack. Nobody sees the body."

"If you say so, Lieutenant."

"I say so. Now, Sam, you better get the hell out of here before the reporters show up and tie you into it."

"Check. That girl, Mona Davis, over at the Borsht house — get her out, but don't tell her what happened to Elsa."

"Anything else?" Bumbera said.

"Yeah . . . thanks, pal." Sam looked down at the blanket for a moment, then left.

# 22

"Hi," said Duchess. "Everything all right?"

"Swell. What do you hear from the Mob?"

"What mob?"

"Skip it. What's up?"

"I hope you don't mind if I work barefoot the rest of the day — felt kind of silly with one shoe on, one shoe off —"

"That's OK."

"Sam, don't you have any female clients who aren't beautiful?"

"Yeah, there's one across the hall that isn't exactly Miss America. Why?"

"Well, there's one in your office that *could* be. She wanted to see you so I shooed her in. A real lady! Is she ever elegant!"

Sam went into the office, knowing who the elegant lady would be.

"Hello, Mr. Marlow," said the elegant Cynthia Ashley. She looked as cool and as beautiful and as perfect as the first time they met.

"Why don't you just call me Sam?"

"Whatever you wish."

"*Whatever?*" Sam made it sound dirty. He

sat down in his swivel chair. "I'll see if I can think something up. Meanwhile, what can I do for you?"

"Nothing really. Mr. Hakim suggested I come round and see you."

"OK, you've seen me — and I've seen you. Now what?"

"Mr. Hakim asked me to tell you that no matter what Alexander Anastas bids, he will better the offer."

"OK. You told me. Now let me ask you something. Do you always do everything Mr. Hakim asks?"

For the first time since last night Cynthia Ashley lost that cool perfect look — but only for an instant.

"Suppose he asked you to sleep with me," said Sam. "Would you do it — or with Zebra or Zinderneuf?"

She rose from the chair, took two steps toward the door, and then turned and walked toward Sam. She stood very close to him. "Until a few years ago there was no Cynthia Ashley. But there *was* a Mary June Janny from a despicable little place in South Carolina you've never heard of — a girl who knew nothing *but* that despicable little place and an even more despicable, boorish, brutish father — a girl who had nothing, but was determined —"

"You can skip the rest of it, Mary June — the whole sad story with the happy ending. Now you've got everything and you'll do anything to keep it as long as you can. Or until you've got enough to kiss him off — if he doesn't kiss you off first. Congratulations on your success — and to what's left of you."

She turned and started to walk out.

"Just a minute — I'm not through." Sam rose and went to her, turned her to him, and stood very close to her. He put both hands on her face.

"You tell your Mr. Hakim to gather up all the cash he's willing to bid. Charter a helicopter and be ready to meet me tomorrow. I'll call him. He'll get his chance. And tell him you persuaded me — just like he thought you would. Goodbye, Mary June, and good luck."

Cynthia Ashley left without saying a word.

Sam got Gena Anastas on the phone. "Hello, Angel. Did you do some thinking?"

"Yes, Sam."

"Me too. That boat of yours — is it seaworthy?"

"Yes. You want to take that trip to China?"

"China comes later. But pick me up at dawn tomorrow — we're going someplace else on the *Veltio Avrio* — and tell the Commodore to get up steam on that minesweeper of his. I'll be in touch — have him gather up all the cash he's willing to spend on the Eyes."

"Sam, I want you to know —"

"We'll have plenty of time to talk when this is over. Pick me up at dawn. So long, Angel."

Duchess came in, barefoot. "He's here again."

"Who?"

"Whats-his-name. Jeeze, he's got clammy hands." She put a hand up to her face. "Sure does smell of perfume. Should I —"

"Yeah. Shoo him in."

Duchess did. Mr. Zebra's eyes were crawling all over her until she left the room.

"Which of the species do you prefer?" Sam asked. "Or can't you make up your mind?"

"Why be restricted in the pleasures of life?"

"Just restrict yourself where she's concerned," Sam said, "or you'll be looking for a good dentist."

"Of course — I never impinge on a stronger man's domain."

"We'll let it go at that."

"Yes, I was most impressed with how you handled Ahman," Mr. Zebra remarked.

"Who the hell is Ahman?"

"Last night at the Blue Fez."

"Oh, you mean that overblown swami with the sword? He was nothing."

"Yes, when you finished with him. Pity you

184

left so early — Miss Ashley's performance
was —"

"Skip it."

"As you wish, of course. I saw her leave
your office just a few moments ago . . ."

"You don't miss much, do you, shorty? All
right, what do you want? I'm gonna have to
start charging you rent."

"Mr. Marlow, did you know that Alexander Anastas has possession of Borsht's letter?"

"Maybe I did and maybe I didn't. Did he
show it to you?"

"Yes, of course."

"Why?"

"He thought I might be of some help."

"But you weren't. Why are you telling
me?"

"Because you and I are partners."

"OK. Why're you backing the Commodore's play?"

"I think we can make a more profitable deal
with him."

"You mean *you* can. Better than the 5 percent from Zinderneuf."

"Of course. A better deal for both you and
me."

"And all that trust Wolfie put in you —
doesn't mean a damn thing when it comes to
business."

"Zinderneuf never really trusted anyone ex-

185

cept his nephew Borsht. He told me that in prison."

"During one of your more intimate moments? OK, Mr. Zebra. Nobody knows the answer to the riddle of the marching men but me."

"You do?!"

"You bet."

"And may I ask what you're going to do next?"

"I'm gonna take a little vacation. Now you stick close to either Anastas or Hakim — I don't care which — and I'll be in touch."

"When?"

"Tomorrow."

"Of course, you know I have been completely candid with you, Mr. Marlow."

"You bet."

"And we *are* partners."

"Check."

"May I inquire where you are vacationing?"

"Sure — Catalina. Now get outa here."

"Of course, of course."

Sam sat and thought for a long, long time. It was a little after six when Duchess came in barefoot, carrying her shoes, and asked if she could leave for the day.

"Yeah," said Sam. "Look, Duchess, I won't be in tomorrow."

"Oh, good," she twittered. "You've been working too hard. You could use a little rest. You're getting bags under your eyes."

Sam took Mustafa Hakim's five-hundred-dollar bill out of his pocket and put it into Duchess's free hand.

"Here. Take it."

"What am I supposed to do with it?"

"Buy yourself some shoes."

"Sam, this is more money than I ever held before."

"Well, don't hold it. Spend it."

"I'll bring you back the change."

"Keep it. You might need it."

"Sam, what're you talking about?"

"Did I ever tell you you were a sweet kid? Now get outa here. Beat it!"

"Good night, Sam."

"Good night, Duchess."

Sam called Bumbera. He was in. Bumbera said that Elsa Borsht had died from an overdose of scopolamine. Evidently somebody had been trying to get her to tell something.

"Yeah," said Sam. "Something she didn't know. Bummy, I'll call you tomorrow. Have a fast boat standing by. You'll get your killer and a lot —"

"Sam, don't try to play a lone hand. Tell me what you know or —"

"Or what? What'll you do — pump me full of scopolamine?"

"There are other ways."

"They won't work."

"Suppose I tail you?"

"Suppose you don't. Look, Bummy, you don't need to tail me. I'll call you in plenty of time."

"Don't take any chances."

"Who *me?* Good night, sweetheart." He hung up.

# 23

Scopolamine. Sam thought about a picture called *The Fallen Sparrow*, 1943, RKO, John Garfield, Maureen O'Hara, and Walter Slezak. Garfield was the sole survivor of a volunteer brigade from the Spanish Civil War. He had what was left of the brigade's battle flag. Slezak, a Nazi, had sworn to get it. Slezak had a limp. He chased Garfield around trying to pump scopolamine into him so he'd tell where the flag was hidden.

Yeah, Garfield, the Golden Boy. He had more expression in his mouth than any other actor before or since. Garfield . . . his last lines in *Body and Soul* to Lloyd Gough, the crooked promoter . . . "What're you gonna do? Kill me? Everybody dies." But Garfield the Golden Boy in real life died too young. Well, Sam might die tomorrow, but not before he wiped out the dirty bastards who killed Elsa Borsht.

He took a hit from the office bottle.

"You drink too much." Mother filled up most of the doorway. She had Linda the cat in one arm and a look on her face that should've been carved on a totem pole. "And who knows what goes on around here between you and that blond sexpot? I saw her leave without any shoes or underwear!"

"Doesn't she wear underwear?"

"You *know* she doesn't."

"Mother, it's strictly business between her and me." Sam gave her a twitch.

"Speaking of business, where's Nicky? And don't try to stall or I'll raise your rent."

"I got a lease."

"I'll break it."

"How?"

"Moral turpitude — between you and that banana-eating blond. I've seen her!"

"There's no clause in the lease says she can't eat bananas."

"We'll see about that — if Nicky's not back in twenty-four hours!" The cat screeched. And Mother slammed the door.

Sam waited about a minute while Mother thumped down the front stairs. He went to the window and watched her walk across the street against a red light. A Toyota screeched to a stop just a few inches from her. Lucky for the Toyota, Sam thought. The driver hollered something at Mother. She paid no attention. Sam figured she probably had poor Nicky on the brain.

Sam closed up the office, then went to the

back stairway leading to the attic. He pushed open the panel and eased through. He made his way toward the light around the corner.

"Hey, Nicky," he said. "It's all right — it's me. Sam Marlow."

"Ah, come in," said Nicky, "come in, come in! I glad you come. I get lonesome . . ."

"Yeah, so's Mother. She was just in to see me. We can't keep on with this stalleroo much longer."

"What this stall-a-roo?"

"The hibernating — is your battery charged yet?"

"What battery?"

"Your machinery, your motor — your strength — you know, the oysters."

"Yeah, sport. I stronger every day. But she big woman!"

"I think she's shrinking."

Nicky beamed. "You mean it?"

"Yeah — losing weight and endurance — pining away for you. She's practically skin and bones — could hardly make it down the stairs. May have to go to bed for a week . . ."

"That what I afraid of."

"No, no. Looks like she's lost her zip."

"Aleetheya?"

"Come again?"

"Truth, aleetheya — truth?"

"Yeah, truth. I think you better come out

by tomorrow night — or she's liable to collapse."

"Okeydoke. You friend. I listen to you."

"Swell."

"But what I tell her? Where I been?"

"Let me do the talking. I'll square it. It'll be OK."

"You friend. I listen. I do what you say."

"Fine. I'll see you tomorrow."

"You stay. We talk. I lonesome. We eat."

"Some other time," said Sam. "I'm allergic to oysters."

Sam drove to his apartment. He went into the bedroom, and just for safekeeping, put the envelope into the post of his brass bed. He didn't think anybody would try anything tonight. They all thought they were going to get the sapphires. He was the only one who knew where the Eyes were, so he was probably safe until he had them in his possession. After that — well, somebody, maybe everybody, would make a play. And so would Sam.

He went into the kitchen, opened a can of chili, and put it on the stove. He drank a bottle of Bud and stirred the pot of chili while it heated.

In a few minutes he took the chili, some crackers, and another bottle of Bud into the living room and turned on the television set.

The early movie was just starting — Dick Powell in *Cornered*. Sam had seen it more than a dozen times but he watched it again. Powell was an ex-flier in World War II. The Nazis had killed his wife in France and he was on their trail. It led to South America and a climactic scene with Luther Adler. Walter Slezak was in this one too. He got his face blown off.

Powell had a habit of running his hand down the front of his suit coat to make sure his tie was tucked in. He got the hell beat out of him five or six times in the picture. What a switch from those musicals he'd made a few years before at Warner's with Ruby Keeler and his ex-wife Joan Blondell. And what a dame that Blondell was.

Sam remembered reading that a duplicate of Blondell's body had been put into a time capsule at the 1939 New York World's Fair. She was supposed to have had the best female figure in the world. Probably a publicity gag — somewhere in the world some girl probably had a better figure — but Blondell's was good enough. *Cornered* was almost over. Right in the middle of Luther Adler's speech about the decadent democracies and how the Nazis would rise again, the phone rang. It was Gena.

"Sam, are you alone?"

"Yeah. Why?"

"Because I'm a jealous woman and I thought you might be keeping company with some beautiful girl —"

"Like who?"

"Like that wild secretary of yours, or Elsa Borsht, or even Cynthia Ashley. I could see the way —"

"No, I'm all alone tonight."

"Then why don't I come over?"

"Sure. At six-thirty in the morning. We got a date to go on a boat ride. I'll be waiting outside."

"Sam, you said we could talk when this is over —"

"Sure — we can do a lot of things, maybe. After tomorrow. See you at six-thirty."

"All right, Sam, if that's the way you want it."

"Want it or not — that's the way it's got to be."

*Cornered* was over. Sam went to bed.

# 24

There are probably more pleasure boats, big and little, berthed alongside the coastline in the Los Angeles area than anyplace else in the world. At least, that's the way it looks along the docks of the Los Angeles Yacht Club in San Pedro.

"Well, there she is," said Gena. "What do you think of her?"

"Like Cary Grant said in *The Philadelphia Story* — she's yar."

"That she is."

"What's a rig like this worth?"

"Two hundred thousand." Gena shrugged.

"That include a full tank of gas?"

"No, that's extra. But the tank *is* full. Where are we going?"

"I'll tell you when we get past the break-water."

"Still the mysterious Mr. Marlow," she smiled.

Two men watched from a parked car as Gena and Sam went aboard.

Ten minutes later the *Veltio Avrio* was

195

heading toward the open sea, with Gena at the helm on the flying bridge and Sam next to her.

"You want to steer?" Gena asked.

"No, thanks — suppose something happened? I wouldn't want to owe you two hundred thousand."

"Actually she's in the name of one of the Commodore's corporations. I don't think the loss would affect the company too much."

"How would it affect you?"

"It would. I love her. But there are different kinds of love. It's just a boat."

"Tell me about it."

"She's a customized Pacemaker — forty-eight feet — sports sedan. Twin diesels — 871 GMC — flying bridge — a saloon and two staterooms forward. She cruises at eighteen knots. Now suppose you tell me where we're going."

"You ever been to Catalina?"

"Been there?" Gena laughed. "Why, I was practically raised there. Is that where we're going?"

"That's the port o'call."

"I own a small house in Avalon."

"It figures. What about wheels?"

"Will a Jeep do?"

"Yeah, that's something I can steer. How long will it take us to get there?"

"Less than two hours."

In an hour and forty minutes the *Veltio Avrio* was in Avalon Bay cruising past the white-columned Casino Ballroom, a towering circular structure that looked down on the crescent-shaped bay, with a perpetual wistful smile, reflecting a million memories of glistening dawns and moonlit nights when lovers danced to the big bands — while far beyond America and across the north Atlantic an endless link of iron ships steamed toward the icy waters of Murmansk, where German submarines sent tubes of death into the helpless hulls of merchant ships and destiny decreed a deep black tomb for cargoes and screaming crews while orchestras ten thousand miles away from there played "Don't Sit under the Apple Tree with Anyone Else but Me" and sailors on leave whisked away their sweethearts under the amber moon of Avalon Bay and made love like it was the end of the world. For some of them it was.

The bay was a sparkling blue semicircle punctuated with boats of variegated colors, sizes, and kinds. Yachts, sloops, and motorboats, some anchored, others churning white wakes across the azure water — overhead, twin-engined seaplanes ferried passengers back and forth from Long Beach and San Pedro to Avalon and Two Harbors.

Five minutes later the *Veltio Avrio* was docked at the Catalina Yacht Club. Sam and Gena walked southwest along Casino Way past the Tuna Club. Sam drew the usual glances and whispers from tourists and natives.

They turned right on Marrilla Avenue and right again on the next street to a Spanish-style two-story house with a WW II Jeep, painted white, parked in the porte cochere.

"The key's in the ignition," Gena said.

"Is it always there?" Sam asked.

"Uh huh."

"Aren't you afraid somebody'll steal it?"

"Where would they go?" Gena smiled.

"You know, you got something there," said Sam. "Say, is there a tool kit around? You know, monkey wrench, hammer, pliers — stuff like that?"

"In the back." She pointed to the Jeep.

"Well then, as Steve McQueen would say — lez go."

They got in. Sam started the engine and steered the Jeep out of the driveway.

"You know how to get to the old Army barracks?" he asked.

"Uh huh, take a right."

Sam did. "You ever been up there?"

"Oh, sure. But the place is all crumbling and falling apart. It really isn't safe. Those buildings are always collapsing."

198

"Built during the Second World War, weren't they?"

"That's right. A Japanese submarine or boat of some kind — so the story goes — fired a couple of shells near Santa Barbara and the Army built a barracks. It's called Fort Cactus — with gun emplacements to sink the Japanese fleet in case they tried to invade Catalina. It seems funny now, doesn't it?"

"Hilarious. Are the cannons still up there?"

"No, just the concrete foundations — but they're on the other side of the barracks. You can't see them unless you climb over the hill. Is that where we're going?"

"Yeah, to the barracks."

"Glad I wore my slacks."

"I kinda like that dress with the slit on the side."

"I would've worn it last night if you had let me come over."

They drove down the narrow paved road for another ten minutes. It was isolated. They didn't see another car or truck coming or going.

"Not much traffic out this way, is there?" said Sam.

"Hardly any."

"What do we do about that?" Sam pointed to a gate across the road ahead.

"It's a bump gate. Slow to about twenty

and hit it. It'll swing open and we drive through."

Sam did. It did and they did. The gate slammed shut behind the Jeep.

A little later Sam pointed. "Look, fugitives from a John Wayne western." A herd of buffalo, more than a hundred, grazed on both sides of the road and up the sloping grassy mountainside.

"There are hundreds here on the island — too many for Catalina to sustain. Cowboys've been rounding them up and shipping them out for years."

"Cowboys? On horseback?"

"That's right. Here's where we turn. Bear to the left."

In another few minutes the paved road turned into a narrow dirt path, twisting and climbing up the mountainside. Past eucalyptus, fig, and ironwood trees — and there, nestling among hundreds of water-starved scrub oaks, Sam could see what was left of Fort Cactus. He shifted gears and the Jeep's tires ground upward over the rutted winding road toward the ghostly garrison.

Five minutes later they were there. Sam got out of the Jeep and helped Gena down. He looked around. It was eerie.

Thirteen, maybe fourteen structures were still standing. Not really standing — leaning, creaking in the wind. Huge wooden earth-anchored galleons, bony pine skeletons, partly covered with peeling black tar paper — most of them roofless, some jutting out from the steep mountain, sustained by slanting wooden stilts angling out of the hard core of earth.

A few of the barracks had been built on what little flat surface was available. It all looked like an old, abandoned movie set. But there had been actual soldiers here during an actual war — probably bored out of their gourd with nothing to do but play cards, shoot craps, listen to Jack Benny, Fibber McGee & Molly, Fred Allen, and Mr. District Attorney on the radio — and gaze at pinups of Betty Grable, Rita Hayworth, Veronica Lake, and Gene Tierney. Some duty — but it beat dodging live ammo.

And here was Sam, standing with a beautiful girl who looked like Gene Tierney, about to latch onto a couple of blue sapphires worth maybe half a million. Some duty. Just so long as he didn't have to dodge live ammo.

"That was the mess hall, I think." Gena pointed.

"Yeah." Sam lifted the tool kit. "Let's walk over this way."

Just off what must have been the main road was a flat concrete base about twenty feet square. On the east side was a hole about eight feet long, three feet wide, and six or seven feet deep.

"This must've been the showers and toilets," Sam said.

"I guess so." Gena shrugged. "But Sam, what are we doing here?"

Sam looked to the east and could see the ocean beyond the winding road that had brought them to Fort Cactus.

"Is there another road up here besides the one we came on?"

"Yes, it forks off down below and comes up from that way."

"Can we see it from here?"

"No, not once you get off Middle Ranch Road."

"OK. Let's not waste any more time."

"What are we doing?"

"We're archaeologists — searching for sapphires."

"Sam! You mean they're *here?*"

"Yeah — ol' Horst Borsht worked on a picture called *The Divers.* It was shot on Catalina about ten years ago. He figured the sapphires would be safer here than in Hollywood. We'll see if he was right."

Sam walked a few steps and stopped in front of the concrete base of what had been the shower and toilet rooms. He stood near another hole, overgrown with weeds and grass — and still visible was the rounded top of a large, buried tank.

Sam took the envelope out of his pocket and handed it to Gena.

"The letter your father managed to get from me was no good without this. I think what we're looking for is right in front of us."

Gena read aloud what Horst Borsht had printed with a fine hand in the small area where the stamp had been.

CATALINA
W. W. II BARRACKS
IN NOZZLE OF
FUEL TANK.

"Sam!" She nearly leaped into the air. "Is this the tank?"

"Should be . . . it's right alongside the road where they probably gassed up."

"Where's the nozzle?"

"Right here. And like I thought, it's all rusted tight." He opened the tool kit, pulled out a wrench and hammer, and began to work on the cap of the nozzle.

"Sam, you really think they're here?"

"They'd better be." He hit the handle of the wrench that was biting into the cap —

once, twice, three times. "I think it's coming."

Sam gripped the wrench handle with both hands and pulled with all he had. The wrench slipped loose from the cap and Sam almost fell over. He locked the jaws of the wrench around the cap and tightened its barrel. He pulled again. The cap began to twist — slowly at first, with rusty particles flaking off, then more easily. It was loosening. Half a dozen more turns and the cap was nearly off. Sam set down the wrench and twisted with both hands until he had the cap off the nozzle and in his hand.

"Oh, Sam, they've just got to be there!"

"Either that — or the Dutchman had some sense of humor. You think there's any rattlesnakes down there?"

"Could there be?" she said with sudden horror.

"I don't know." He smiled. "They like cool, shady places."

"Sam, what're we going to do?"

"We didn't come this far to worry about a little ol' rattlesnake or two." Sam picked up a piece of wood about twelve inches long and poked it into the mouth of the nozzle. The stick came to a stop about six or seven inches deep.

"No rattlesnakes." Sam smiled again. "Well, Angel, I don't think my paw'll fit down there. Should we leave — or do you want to try?"

"Cross your fingers," she said, and reached into the narrow passage. "Sam, there's something there. A little case or something."

"Yeah. He probably stuffed some wadding in the nozzle and put the Eyes on top of it."

"I've got it!" She withdrew her slender arm. Her little fist was smudged with rust and dirt, but she was holding a metal container.

"Here, Sam — you open it." The metal container was two inches across, four inches long, more than two inches deep. It was heavy for its size.

"No, Angel — you go ahead."

Gena took a deep breath. "I'm — Sam — I'm trembling."

"So am I. Open the damn thing."

She did. There, resting on a white velvet lining, were the two most perfectly matched blue sapphires in the world, the last sight ever seen by the eyes of Alexander the Great. And the sapphires did look like eyes — huge and deep and mysterious. As if they had seen what no other eyes had ever seen. As if they knew their worth — and their danger. Almost as if they were alive.

"My God," Gena said, "I've never seen anything like them. They're — they're frightening. Sam, I'm scared. Let's get out of here."

"Sure."

"You take them," she said.

"OK." He did.

"Sam." There among the derelict buildings, with broken walls and caved-in ceilings around them, where lonely soldiers had dreamed of Rita Hayworth, Veronica Lake, and Betty Grable just twenty-two miles across the dark Pacific, Sam and Gena now stood — with one of the great treasures of all ages in their possession. She whispered, "Sam, you trusted me," and kissed him.

"Why not?" he said. "What could you do? Kill me? Everybody dies."

That's when the black sedan started toward them. It had been parked among the scrub oaks forty or fifty yards away, at the end of the secondary road. Two men had waited in the car. One of them, Buster, had watched with binoculars while Gena and Sam had retrieved the sapphires. And now the car roared toward them, and Buster held a .38 revolver out the window, pointed at Sam.

The first shot whistled past Sam's ear. He thrust the case with the sapphires into his pocket, pulled out the Luger, fired three rounds at the approaching sedan, and pushed Gena toward the cover of one of the gutted barracks. A couple more shots from Buster kicked up a clump of dirt near Gena's feet and splintered the frame of the doorless doorway of the barracks as Sam and Gena ducked inside.

The sedan braked to a dusty stop. Buster and the driver jumped out, spitting lead from their .38s. Neither was wearing a ski mask. That meant they weren't worried about being identified — it also meant they didn't intend to leave any living witnesses. But Sam had other ideas. He led Gena stumbling across the warped and buckling floor toward the back door of the barracks.

They had just made the rear exit when the two gunmen appeared at the front door. Sam shoved Gena down the sagging stairs, turned, and slammed four slugs at the gunmen, who ducked back and returned his fire. The blasts spattered around and through the rear doorway just as Sam dove out.

As he led Gena across the cover of rocks and trees behind the barracks the driver shot at them through one of the glassless windows. Buster came out the back way, gun blazing. On the run, Sam fired at both gunmen, then pushed another clip into his Luger as they reached the relative safety of another drooping building.

"We got to get to that Jeep," said Sam to a breathless Gena. "When we do I'll hand you the Luger — you ever shoot a gun?"

"Yes." Gena nodded.

"Good. Come on." He took her hand and they ran through the slanting skeletal structure.

"Watch out!" said Sam. There was a gaping hole in the floor. They made their way around it and ran almost to the front door, where the Jeep was parked.

Buster was coming in the back doorway; the driver ran along the outside of the building trying to head them off. When Sam and Gena got to the front stairway of the barracks Sam pumped a volley of shots at the driver. He dove behind a rock. Buster was running through the barracks firing and didn't see the hole on the floor until it was too late. He fell about ten feet and landed on the hard slanting ground below.

Sam made it to the Jeep, still throwing lead at the driver. Gena jumped into the back as Sam started the Jeep. He handed her the Luger.

"Keep shooting!"

The driver scrambled toward the sedan, firing, as Buster crawled out from under the barracks. By the time Sam made a sharp U-turn both gunmen were in the sedan.

Sam pushed the accelerator to the floor and the Jeep raced ahead. Gena got off a few shots, which hit nothing. But the sedan revved up, turned, and came in pursuit.

Sam scraped the side of the Jeep across the props of a sagging building, ripping away the foundation — the entire building collapsed just behind them, barricading the road and blocking the path of the sedan. But it didn't take long for the driver to maneuver around the wreckage and get back on the dirt road.

Sam slowed the Jeep for just a moment. "Get in the front seat before you fall out!" Gena climbed into the front and Sam gunned ahead. It was downhill but the road snaked left and right and Sam had to spin the steering wheel accordingly. One mistake and the Jeep would fly off the narrow, winding road and into one of the steep canyons below. Whoever was driving the sedan knew his business — he was keeping pace with the Jeep.

Any gunplay along the serpentine road would be futile. Both vehicles dipped, bounced, and swayed, their wheels churning trails of dirt and dust. Then they were almost to the base of the mountain where the dirt road turned to macadam. Sam made the last sharp curve and the Jeep's wheels rolled onto the pavement with the sedan a couple of hundred yards behind.

Sam hit the floor with the accelerator, but the sedan was faster. Ahead was the herd of buffalo — one of the beasts stood stolidly in the middle of the road, with no notion of moving. Sam beeped the horn but the buffalo ignored the warning. At the last moment Sam curved the Jeep off the road and around the insouciant buffalo. The sedan followed Sam's path off and on the narrow vein of pavement. The buffalo paid them no mind.

"Sam!" Gena screamed as they turned a corner. "Slow down!" She pointed to the bump gate. Sam hit the brake. The Jeep had decelerated to thirty-five by the time they smashed into the gate, but it was too fast — the impact almost tossed both of them out of the Jeep.

Just as the gate slammed shut behind them the sedan crashed into it, doing at least forty. The shock spun the rear end of the sedan off the road sideways, killing the engine. But the driver was a real pro. He had it started and back on the road in six seconds.

The macadam path began to climb and wind up another steep mountain. But the curves weren't as sharp, and Sam could make good speed — fifty, sixty, seventy. There was a sign to the right — INDIAN BURIAL GROUND AHEAD. They were getting closer to the ocean.

They passed the burial ground near the rim of the beetling cliff. Sam spotted a stance of scrub oaks that went almost to the cliff's edge, completely obscuring the view to the left. He veered the Jeep off the road and raced parallel along the line of heavy foliage. The sedan was gaining, and the cliff's edge, with the sea a hundred yards below, came up fast. There was only ten feet between the last tree and the end of the cliff.

The Jeep almost went over the cliff as Sam spun a sharp left just past the last tree. He circled back fast through the foliage and came up behind the sedan, which was slowing as it approached the lip of the cliff. Sam's foot hit the floorboard and the Jeep hit the back of the sedan — and the sedan scudded and skidded off the rim. Sam and Gena could hear both men scream as the sedan rolled over and plummeted down — down, bouncing and scraping along the jagged wall of the cliff and into the wine-dark waters of the sea below.

# 25

Half an hour later Sam had made three telephone calls from Gena's house in Avalon to the mainland — to Commodore Alexander Anastas, to Mustafa Hakim, and to Lt. Marion Bumbera. Gena walked in from the kitchen with two cups of hot black coffee.

"The report just came over KBRT."

"What report?"

"About the rented car going off the cliff at Little Harbor. No survivors."

"That's terrible," Sam said.

"My heart's still in my throat."

"Everything's jake, Angel. Drink your coffee. We got to get going."

"Where to now?"

"Exactly ten miles northeast of Casino Point."

"But Sam, there's nothing out there."

"No. But there will be."

"What?"

"All the parties who are interested in these." Sam opened the case and set it on a table. The Eyes gleamed as they caught the sunlight coruscating through the window.

"I hate them," Gena said. "They've caused nothing but misery and death."

"Don't blame them, Angel. They're just a couple of stones. It's not their fault."

"Who do they belong to, Sam?"

"That's what we're going to find out." Sam pulled the empty clip out of the Luger. "Drink your coffee."

"Sam, it's all my fault. I got you into this."

"No. I was already in. You just pulled me under a little deeper."

"You know, Sam — you never did tell me why you hit me that time in Cane's Club."

"John Wayne slugged his pal Ward Bond in *Hondo* for the same reason."

"Well, what is it?"

"Simple. When you want to confuse the enemy, hit a friend."

"I see. I think. . . . About those pictures —"

"Forget it. We'll talk about it when this is over — if there's anything to talk about."

# 26

Ten miles northeast of Casino Point, a little less than halfway to the California coast from Avalon, the converted minesweeper *Eurydice*, now the luxury yacht of Commodore Alexander Anastas, came into view of the *Veltio Avrio*.

"Go ahead," said Sam. Gena was at the helm of the smaller ship. "Pull alongside." Gena maneuvered her ship around and floated close to the *Eurydice*.

Anastas, his wife, and George looked down from the rail. Anastas waved. "Mr. Marlow. Good to see you, sir! Come aboard!"

"Oh, no," Sam hollered back. "That's not the way it's gonna be. *You* come aboard. With the green!"

"Very well, sir. As you wish."

Some of the crew of the *Eurydice* lowered a small motor launch and brought it around to the ladder alongside the hull of the huge ship. George climbed down first, carrying a suitcase, then helped the massive Commodore as he lumbered his way down the ladder and into the bobbing launch.

The small boat cruised across the short span of water from the *Eurydice* to the *Veltio Avrio* and Sam tossed them a line. George climbed aboard first with the suitcase. Then he turned to assist the Commodore, who huffed and heaved his way aboard.

"Ahh," said the Commodore, "thank you, thank you," and took the suitcase from George. Just as he did Sam's right hand lashed out and hit George a karate chop slightly below the ear, knocking him off the deck and into the sea.

"That squares us for the garage," said Sam.

"By heaven," the Commodore laughed, "you *are* something. No hard feelings, I hope."

"My feelings are just fine, Commodore. Now after your boys fish him out, have them pull that glorified gunboat of yours away from us while we transact our business."

"Yes." The Commodore looked to the men in the launch, who were already helping the groggy, soggy George into the small boat. "You heard what he said. Tell Captain Adams to pull away." The Commodore looked back at Sam. "Is that satisfactory, sir?"

"Just dandy," said Sam.

"You *do* have the sapphires, do you not, Mr. Marlow?"

"All in good time, Commodore. We're expecting more guests."

Just then a jet ranger helicopter arched into view from the direction of the mainland. The Commodore's jowls shuddered. "Who is it? Who's up there?"

"Just your old partner and some other interested parties."

"But you said you were selling the sapphires to *me* —"

"No, I said you could *bid* on them. You shouldn't mind a little competition, Commodore — makes for a healthier market."

The helicopter made its descent and the wash from its propellers sent shimmering white ripples across the water all around the *Veltio Avrio*. The Commodore, suitcase in his big hand, went into the saloon grumbling something that sounded like "sonofabitch" — and something more that was drowned out by the roar of the dipping helicopter.

The pilot brought the big bird slowly and smoothly closer to the *Veltio Avrio* until the helicopter hovered inches above the foredeck of the ship. From out of the helicopter stepped Mustafa Hakim as easily as if he were walking off a curb. He too carried a suitcase. Hakim was followed by Wolf Zinderneuf, Mr. Zebra, and Cynthia Ashley.

The man in blue waved and the jet ranger lifted straight up, dipped its nose, and roared away.

Hakim, followed by his entourage, walk toward Sam. "I brought the money — and the others, as you asked, although why you wanted them here —"

"Why not?" said Sam. "They've all got a vested interest in the deal."

By now the *Eurydice*, carrying out her captain's orders, was heading farther away from the *Veltio Avrio*.

"Come on." Sam motioned. "Let's all go inside. You too, Angel," he hollered to Gena, still at the helm. "Just let her drift." Sam watched as they all walked into the saloon. Mr. Zebra waited until the rest had gone in and whispered to Sam, "Remember, we are partners. Half and half."

"Of course," said Sam.

# 27

"All right, folks — everybody take a seat and make yourself comfortable." Sam sat on the edge of a table toward the front of the saloon.

Commodore Anastas and Mustafa Hakim gripped their suitcases and glowered at one another. Sam took the small metal case out of his coat pocket and set it on the table next to him. Then he lifted the Luger out of his pocket and set it next to the case.

"I guess you boys are entitled to see the merchandise before the bidding starts." He opened the case and held it in front of him. Everyone in the room leaned forward for a better look — everyone except Gena.

"Here they are, folks. Just a couple of blue stones. But there aren't any others like 'em in the whole world, and never were — makes 'em kind of special. Take a good look, but keep your hands in plain sight. We don't want any more funerals."

"I must have them," said the Commodore.

"They're even bluer than I had imagined," said Hakim.

"I've waited over thirty years," said Wolf Zinderneuf.

"We'll see what you get for your trouble," Sam replied. "They cost your nephew his life. Some other people paid the same price. Now then, Commodore, Mr. Hakim, would you boys consider splitting the set? Buying one apiece?"

"No," said Hakim.

"Never," said the Commodore.

"I didn't think so," said Sam.

"May I, Mr. Marlow — just for a moment — may I hold them in my hands?" The Commodore stuck out both his beefy palms. "Please?"

"Sure — you can even squeeze 'em. They won't spoil." Sam picked up the sapphires as if they were a couple of marbles kids might play with and dropped one into each of the Commodore's quivering palms. Anastas closed both fists and breathed deeply. His huge frame shuddered as if a shock were going through his system. Then he opened both palms and brought the sapphires close to his eyes.

"The Eyes of Alexander," he intoned. "My eyes. I must have them."

"You got a shot at 'em. How about you, Mr. Hakim — want to heft 'em once?"

"Yes. Please."

Sam took the sapphires from the Commodore's cold, quivering hands and walked over to Hakim. "Here you go." Mustafa Hakim took both sapphires in one hand. His lips trembled as he spoke. "Bluer than anything on earth —"

"And heaven and hell too, probably. OK, boys. That's enough sampling the merchandise." Sam took back the sapphires and placed them in the metal case. Then he sat down on the edge of the table again.

"Now then — I may want to do some fast traveling when this is over, so I'll only take what you have on you. I believe the last official bid was one hundred fifty thousand from the Commodore."

"One seventy-five," said Hakim.

"Two hundred thousand," said the Commodore.

"A quarter of a million," said Hakim.

"Well now, that's some pretty spirited bidding, boys. I like that. All right, where were we?"

"Three hundred thousand," said the Commodore.

"Three hundred fifty thousand," said Hakim.

Cynthia Ashley cleared her throat.

"Were you bidding, lady?" Sam inquired.

Cynthia shook her head no. "But you are

enjoying it, I hope. Thought you'd get a kick out of this. That's why I asked Mr. Hakim to bring you along. Now, the last bid was —"

"Four hundred thousand," the Commodore grumbled.

"Good," said Sam. "But not good enough."

"Four-fifty," said Hakim.

"Better." Sam smiled.

"Half a million!" The Commodore rose from his chair.

"Sit down, Commodore. You're rocking the boat. Now you gentlemen understand that this is a cash transaction. Don't bid more than you have with you."

"Six hundred thousand!" Mustafa Hakim wiped his tongue across his thin blue lips.

"We're getting up there," Sam said. "Pretty soon we'll separate the sheep from the goat."

"Mr. Marlow —"

"Yes, Commodore?"

"Seven hundred."

"Seven hundred — *thousand?*" Sam smiled.

"Yes!"

"OK. Duly noted. Is that it?"

Wolf Zinderneuf moved his wooden arm across his lap with his good right hand and adjusted the rest of his body in the chair.

"What do you think, Wolfie? Not bad, huh? Course we haven't talked about how we're going to split up the pot yet — but then, I don't think the bidding is over. Or is it, Mr. Hakim?"

"Three-quarters of a million," said Hakim.

"Uh huh — now that *is* seven hundred fifty thousand, isn't it?" Sam said. "Yeah, sure it is. Just as sure as four quarters make a buck."

"Eight hundred thousand!" said the Commodore.

"Eight-fifty!" said Hakim.

"Nine!" said the Commodore.

"Nine-fifty!" said Hakim.

"Mr. Marlow." The Commodore stood again. "I have *one million dollars* in this suitcase —"

Hakim also stood. "And *I* have a million here."

"Well, well," said Sam. "Are you boys telling me each of you is bidding a million dollars for the doodads?"

"Yes," said Hakim.

"Correct," said the Commodore.

"OK, let's open up the suitcases. I'd like to see the color of that cash."

Both men went to the table, set down their suitcases, and opened them. Both were filled with currency.

"Well," said Sam, "it looks like it'll spend all right. Close 'em up, boys. Wouldn't want a sudden gust of wind to blow any of it away, like in *The Treasure of the Sierra Madre*. Now, seems like we got a standoff. So who's gonna sweeten the pot? Just with what you have on you, boys."

"I probably have another two thousand in cash," said Hakim.

"I'll tell you what," said Sam. "Each of you put his suitcase on the floor in front of you."

They did.

"I may have another two thousand on me, sir," the Commodore said.

"OK — why don't you each put all the cash you have on top of your suitcases?"

Both men emptied their wallets and set the cash on the cases.

"Yeah," said Sam. "I'd say you're pretty close to being even. You know, Mr. Hakim, that's a real nice diamond ring you wear. Of course it's not as blue as the sapphires —"

"This ring is worth more than fifteen thousand dollars."

"That hikes your pot," said Sam. "That is, if you're willing to include it."

"Yes." Hakim took the ring off his finger and placed it on his suitcase.

"I too have a ring, Mr. Marlow, worth at least as much." The Commodore put his ring on his suitcase.

"A gold watch — Patek Philippe — seven thousand." Hakim added it to his pile.

"Uh huh." Sam nodded. "What about you, Commodore? You got a watch?"

The Commodore grunted and removed a thin gold watch from his thick hairy wrist.

"Well, boys — I'd say you're neck and neck coming down the stretch."

"These cuff links are also blue diamonds," said Hakim. "Value at least four thousand."

"Very good — looks like that puts the team from the East ahead."

"My diamond stickpin, sir. Worth easily as much." The Commodore placed the diamond pin on his pile.

"Not quite, Commodore." Sam shook his head. "But let me ask you — are those real gold buttons on that blazer of yours?"

"Yes."

"Well, take it off and toss it on the pile — that'll pull you up even."

"Look here, sir, you're going too far. I'm not willing to be —"

"OK then — don't. You're out!" said Sam. "That makes Hakim's bid —"

"Just a moment — I'm in! *I'm in!*"

"Good," said Sam. "Good. Now look — let's quit wasting time. All that stuff you two fellows are wearing is worth plenty — silk ties and shirts, alligator belts, lizardskin shoes. Go ahead — take all that stuff off and toss it on the pile so I can estimate —"

"What do you think you're doing?" Hakim snarled. "Who do you think you're dealing with? I won't play the fool for you or —"

"OK, then quit — and *you're out!* The sapphires'll go to the Commodore. That'll be it. Either that or both of you strip to your shorts while I make up my mind!"

"Get these people out of here," said Hakim, but the Commodore was already clumsily removing his clothes as if he were anxiously preparing to go to bed with a beautiful woman.

"Oh, no. They've got to stay. We still have a couple of things to settle — like murder. Go ahead, Mr. Hakim — down to your shorts. You got nothing to be ashamed of. A man like you who rarely drinks or smokes — you ought to be in pretty good shape." Sam winked at Cynthia Ashley and said, "How y'all doin', Mary June?" Nobody but she and Sam got it. But nobody was supposed to. Mary June smiled a faint, perfect smile.

Both men undressed as the others watched. Two titans — two of the richest, most powerful men alive — stripping nearly naked for the privilege of bidding as much over a million as each could assemble on a pile in front of him.

"Mr. Marlow," the Commodore said, taking off his enormous trousers. "This ship is mine. I will include —"

"Commodore," said Gena, "you wouldn't. Yes — yes, I guess you would. You always have — you've done *anything* to get what you want."

"The boat won't float, Commodore — not in this deal. I only take what I can carry with me."

Mustafa Hakim was down to his blue shorts and socks — he was much scrawnier than he appeared in his tailored blue suits. But there in his underwear he had a thought. "Mr. Zebra," he said, "you have cash on you — let me have it. I'll —"

"No — the loan won't float either," said Sam. "But funny you should ask, him of all people. OK, boys — that's good enough. Now go sit in your chairs while I mull this over."

The Commodore, wearing only bloomer-type shorts and dark glasses, lumbered to his chair like an old elephant and sat himself down. Hakim, adorned only in bikinilike silk blue shorts, walked to his chair, sat, and crossed his spindly legs.

"Well, Wolfie," said Sam. He glanced at his watch. "While I decide on who gets the sapphires, let's talk about murder. Now, that nephew of yours. He was loyal to the last — couldn't be persuaded to double-cross you.

"Somebody hired some goons to try. There

were four of them to begin with. Two of 'em
— Buster and Nero's Uncle — showed up at
the Hollywood Bowl when Elsa, who didn't
even know about the sapphires, was telling
me about her father's troubles. Maybe the
goons thought she had the stones on her —
that she was slipping 'em to me — or that I
was slipping 'em to her. Anyhow, they decided to search us. I decided they wouldn't.
So Nero's Uncle ended up with a wounded
wing.

"The next night he took it on himself to
come after me. But meanwhile the other two
goons were trying to put the snatch on Borsht
and bring him to whoever hired them. It was
getting close to the deadline. But Borsht had
other ideas. He pulled a gun and the goon
shot Borsht. I shot the goon. That got my
name and picture in the paper. So everybody
wanted to hire me. That's when you walked
in — isn't it, Angel?"

Gena nodded. "Yes, that's right, Sam. I've
tried to tell you since then —"

"You didn't have to tell me. I knew the
story about the pictures was pure cock and
bull — wasn't it, Commodore?"

Alexander Anastas adjusted his dark
glasses. "Merely a case of a dutiful daughter
helping her father . . ."

"You took the oblique approach, huh,

Commodore? Figured I'd fall for a beautiful damsel in distress and you'd find out what I knew about the sapphires. Had it all rigged with Cane and that phony jock with some fake pictures I was never supposed to see. But it didn't play that way."

"Sam," said Gena. "You knew — all this time?"

"I rarely correspond with my conscience," Sam answered. "I wanted to be a gentleman — but I couldn't forget I was a detective. While the three of you were laid out in Cane's office I took a squint at the torn photos — they were of you all right, but more like graduation pictures than pornography. But if that's the way you and the Commodore wanted to play it, it was OK with me. Specially when you showed up at the apartment."

"Sam — please."

"You were still working for the Commodore — maybe he promised you a bigger boat, or an airplane, or a small kingdom someplace. I don't know. But you knew I had Borsht's letter; you saw me put it in my pocket. When you couldn't find it that night the Commodore sicced George onto me in the garage. He got it, all right, but the trouble was the Commodore couldn't figure out the riddle of the marching men."

"I have already apologized for that incident,

sir," said the Commodore. "But I did not hire the man who killed Borsht."

"I didn't say you did, Commodore. But whoever did hire the goons had them go back to Borsht's house and do some searching. When that didn't work one of them imitated me on the phone to Elsa. They tried to get her to tell something she didn't know — and that cost her her life."

There were gasps all over the room.

"That's right," said Sam. "And somebody's gonna pay for it. But who? You, Commodore? Gena? Hakim? Cynthia? Zinderneuf? Zebra? Who?"

Sam picked up the Luger. His hand swept across the room. "*Who?*" he repeated. Then he pointed the Luger directly at Zebra. "Being an agent for five percent wasn't good enough, was it? You wanted at least half — and a hundred percent if you could get rid of me!"

"*Huenden!*" screamed Zinderneuf. He rose and with his good hand smacked Mr. Zebra across the mouth.

"Girls! Girls!" said Sam. "Let's control ourselves. I wouldn't want this thing to go off in all the excitement. Now sit down, Wolfie. You make me nervous."

Zinderneuf mumbled something else in German and sat down.

"OK, Mr. Zebra — let's get back to your game plan. Instead of just acting as agent you told Anastas you yourself would deliver the sapphires. And Commodore — you didn't care who got them to you, just so you got them. What did you do? Have George tail Zebra and find out he was seeing a lot of Borsht?"

"That is correct, sir."

"But you, Mr. Z., couldn't persuade Borsht to double-cross his uncle the commanding officer — and you knew Zinderneuf would be in L.A. the next day with Hakim. What were you finally gonna do — snatch Borsht and dose him with scopolamine?"

Mr. Zebra sat staring at Sam, saying nothing.

"Borsht wrote the letter to himself," Sam went on, "figuring if anything happened to him sooner or later Elsa would solve the riddle — maybe with Zinderneuf's help, maybe not. I'm not sure. But Borsht *didn't* know she'd hire a private detective and turn it over to him.

"And you, Mr. Zebra — you slipped again. First you told me you didn't know Borsht was Zinderneuf's nephew. But later you mentioned that in prison Zinderneuf had told you he didn't trust anyone — *except* his nephew. That's when I started narrowing it all down to

230

you. You're the only one I told I was going to Catalina. Even Gena didn't know — we were just going for a boat ride — but those two goons of yours knew. They took the plane to Catalina and were there in twenty minutes with a rented car ready to tail us. They're still there. Very still."

"Sam," Gena said in a pleading voice, "you've got to believe I didn't know that Zebra hired those men . . ."

"Sure you didn't. Hell, they would've killed you, too. Did you know *that,* Commodore?"

"To ask a question such as that, sir," the Commodore said, "you must have a very low opinion of me."

"It's low, all right," Sam said, "but not quite that low. Not as low as my opinion of Mr. Zebra."

Mr. Zebra finally spoke. "Who cares about your opinion?" he said cynically. "Would a jury believe you — with your made-over face, and that outrageous voice and costume? In the quaint vernacular of your country, Mr. Marlow, you are screwy."

"Maybe I am, Mr. Zebra. But maybe not as screwy as you and your kind think. Maybe this is all part of a disguise — a mask to throw the enemy off guard, lower his defenses, make him say and do things he wouldn't ordinarily — and wind up like you're gonna wind up.

231

Did you ever think about that?"

"Of course, you'll have a difficult time proving any of this," Zebra smirked.

"Maybe — but everybody here knows it. I think a jury would know it too. In my office we talked about splitting the profits into thirds with Elsa. But just before we came in here you said fifty-fifty. Nobody else that's still alive knew Elsa was dead. You killed her — and you're gonna get knocked over for it."

Sam put the Luger back on the table. He picked up the open case with the sapphires.

"What about those?" Hakim asked.

"Yes," joined the Commodore. "Who gets the Eyes?"

"They are mine," Zinderneuf shrieked. "I've given thirty years of my life!"

Sam walked around to the rear of the table, closing the metal case. He looked at his watch, then set the case back on the table.

"They're evidence. It's up to Lieutenant Bumbera to decide. He'll be here any minute — I called him, too."

"They are mine!" Zinderneuf repeated.

"Sir, can't we make some other arrangement?" the Commodore suggested.

"Yes," Hakim agreed. "Something can be worked out."

"No. I don't think so. It's too late." Sam looked at his watch again, then put both his hands in his coat pockets.

"Sam." Gena rose.

"Yes, Angel." Sam took a step toward her and it happened fast.

Mr. Zebra sprang for the Luger and got it. He pointed it at Sam and fired. It seemed he couldn't miss, but Sam pulled the derringer out of his pocket and shot Zebra directly between the eyes. A comical expression of bewilderment came across Mr. Zebra's face for an instant — then he fell dead. But Zinderneuf was on his feet. He grabbed the metal case with his good hand, shoved the table into Sam, picked up the fallen Luger, and quickly managed to transfer the case to the grip of his wooden hand. He vaulted for the door, knocking Hakim down. He turned and fired the Luger wildly, then ran out of the saloon and onto the deck. Sam pushed past the Commodore and Hakim, just getting to his feet.

As Sam came out the door Zinderneuf scampered toward the foredeck — but he was running out of boat. Sam picked up a heavy coil of rope. He saw the Port Police boat in the distance coming out of the east, sweeping toward the setting sun and the *Veltio Avrio*. Bumbera, Hacksaw, and several others were on the bow of the charging police boat.

Anastas, Hakim, Gena, and Cynthia came out of the saloon. They stayed on the lower deck while Sam started toward Zinderneuf. Zinderneuf held the Luger in his right hand and had the metal case locked in the curled grip of the artificial limb.

Sam moved closer and Zinderneuf pointed the Luger at him.

"Sam!" Gena implored, "don't! He'll kill you!"

But Sam moved steadily ahead. "Give it up, Nazi. You got no place to go."

"Never!" Zinderneuf cried. "They belong to me. Thirty years of my life —"

Suddenly Sam threw the coil of rope. Zinderneuf fired at the same time, but the rope hit him hard across the face. He fell backward off the ship and into the ocean.

It seemed as if Commodore Anastas and Mustafa Hakim, both nearly naked, were about to dive in after the thrashing Zinderneuf who still gripped the sapphires — but they both saw it at the same time. So did everyone else.

The great dorsal fin of the huge white shark sliced toward Zinderneuf, flailing atop the water. Zinderneuf saw it and screamed. The police couldn't shoot for fear of hitting the terrified man — and the gaping jaws of the white monster hit and closed, tearing off Zinderneuf's arm. The shark dove deep and disappeared.

Zinderneuf had passed out from the shock. Two of the policemen jumped in to retrieve the unconscious man while Bumbera, Hacksaw, and the others pointed their revolvers at the water in case the shark came back for more.

The two nearly naked men on the deck of the *Veltio Avrio* looked at each other.

"Could you tell which arm the shark got?" the Commodore asked.

"Yes," Hakim replied sadly. "The one with the sapphires."

"Damn," said the Commodore softly.

Sam tossed a line to Bumbera, then jumped aboard the police boat. Zinderneuf lay on the deck.

"God almighty," said one of the policemen. "His arm's missing but there's no blood."

"That shark had to be twenty feet long," Bumbera exclaimed. "Swallowed his arm like it was a string bean. Jaws as big as . . ."

"Yeah," said Sam. "There've been a lot of those sharks around lately. I guess my Luger got lost at sea, huh?"

"Forget the Luger," said Bumbera. "Sam, what the hell is going on?"

"The guy who killed Elsa Borsht is on that ship." Sam pointed to the *Veltio Avrio*.

"I don't suppose he's alive," Bumbera said.

"No," Sam replied. "I'll explain it all to you on the way back."

"Sure, Sam. But would you just explain one thing right now?"

"Of course," said Sam, the way Mr. Zebra used to say it.

Bumbera pointed to the Commodore and Hakim. "Why are those two men standing there without any clothes on?"

# 28

Journeys end in lovers meeting — it was a tender, touching, poignant reunion. At eight-thirty that night Mother thumped up the stairs and through the door marked:

SAM MARLOW
Private Investigator
"I Don't Sleep"

Mother had come in response to Duchess's phone call, per Sam's instructions. She carried Linda in her arms and her face still looked like an iron mask — until she saw Nicky.

Mr. Kalamavrakinopoulos sat in a chair with a bemused look on the face of his bandaged head. A pair of crutches leaned next to him against the chair.

"Nicky! Honey pot!" The iron mask melted into a blazon of sweet concern. "What happened?" She started toward him.

"Easy, Mother," said Sam, stepping between them. "You can see he's not fully recovered."

"Oh, my poor baby," Mother cooed. "Tell Mother all about it."

Nicky looked at Sam for help.

"He's gonna be all right," said Sam. "There was an accident. Hit and run. Poor ol' Nick here lost his memory — wandered around for days in a daze — till his memory came back."

"Oh, the poor baby —" Mother sucked in her breath.

"It was terrible. He's also suffered internal injuries," Sam added.

"Oh, no," she gasped.

"Yeah. And there's damage to his groin —"

"Good God! You mean —"

"You'll have to be gentle, Mother — warm baths, tender loving care — like Florence Nightingale. You'll have to nurse him back to health."

"I will! I will!"

"Sure you will. The bandages can come off tonight, but he'll need plenty of rest —"

"You're a first-class detective, Mr. Marlow. I'll tell all the girls at the gym."

"Swell."

Mother walked over to Nicky, dropped the cat to the floor, took the crutches in one hand, and lifted Nicky with the other. "Come on, honey pot," she said. "We're going home." Nick put his arms around Mother and nodded. As they started out of the office she turned to Sam.

"You get three months' free rent — that was our deal — but just watch what goes on around here between you and Miss Banana."

Mother carried Nicky out of the office. The cat screeched and followed them.

"What did she mean by that?" Duchess inquired. The phone rang. Duchess walked over to Sam's desk and picked up the receiver. "Hi." There was a pause. "Yes, this is I." Another pause. "You're going to do what? Oh, you poor thing . . . oh, no, I don't think . . . wait till I get a pencil . . ." Sam took the phone from her and put it back on the cradle.

"Sam, I'm telling you that poor fellow needs help," Duchess said.

"Yeah," Sam replied, "don't we all. Thanks for sticking around, Duchess."

"That's all right. I hope you enjoyed your day off."

"It was swell. Go home, Duchess."

"Oh — I'm not going home. I've got a date with a musician. A tuba player."

"Have fun," said Sam.

"We will," she twittered. "Good night."

"Good night, Duchess."

Sam took a hit from the office bottle.

# 29

There was an ache in Sam's gut as he walked up the stairs to his apartment. It had all happened in less than a week — a lot of dead men ago. But the ache wasn't for them. It was for Elsa. She'd been the real innocent in the piece, and she was dead. All because of a couple of stones she never even saw. Poor Elsa. Bury the dead — life is for the living. But the ache was still there.

He opened the door to his apartment and went in. He knew even before he closed the door. He walked across the room and stood for a moment looking at the thin sliver of light between the carpet and the bedroom door. He knocked softly — once, twice, three times. Then he went in.

She was in the big brass bed, her beautiful face and hair easily resting against the pillow propped on the headboard. Those eyes — a little Chinese — hair black as a raven's wing. The perfect curve of her patrician nose. Skin white as snow on a twenty-thousand-foot peak. That lovely red, red mouth, with teeth a little too large but white and sweet as sugar.

The thin, soft sheet outlined her nakedness. Only her arms, long and pliant, were outside the sheet. She held a book in her hands.

"What're you doing, Angel?"

"Waiting for somebody."

"Anybody in particular?"

"I'm very particular."

"How'd you get in?"

"I have connections."

"Yeah, I remember."

"Sam, how did it go with Bumbera?"

"He's pretty mad. Not as mad as Hacksaw. But they'll get over it. What're you reading?"

"One of the books from your library. It's called *The Maltese Falcon*. I'd never read it before."

"The girl goes to jail in the end."

"Sam — I never meant for anyone to get hurt."

"I did."

"Do you want to hurt me?"

Sam walked over to the nightstand. Gena had poured some Grand Marnier from the bottle into two glasses. He picked up the glasses and gave one to Gena. "Confusion to the enemy."

"Sam, why did you let Zebra get to your gun? He could've killed you."

"Not with blanks. That's something else I

241

didn't tell Bumbera."

"But why?"

"Because I didn't know if a jury would convict him."

"So you were the jury."

"And the executioner."

He started to undress. She sipped the brandy.

"Sam — all I tried to do was help an old man — my father — before he went blind."

"He'll still have Teresa. That ain't bad. And all she has to do is keep on paying her dues — like Mary June Janny."

"Who?"

"Never mind. How's the Commodore taking it?"

Gena smiled. "I think both he and Hakim are getting ready to go fishing — for shark."

"They'll be wasting their time." Sam took the two sapphires out of his coat pocket and tossed them onto the bed. The cold blue stones gleamed against the white sheet.

"Sam! My God! I thought the shark got them!"

"Not that shark."

"But how?"

"I palmed them when I closed the case. I didn't want some maniac to grab them and run."

"What are you going to do with them?"

"I don't know yet. I would've given them to Elsa. Maybe you still want them. The last time you were up here that's what you were trying . . ."

"Do you really believe that?"

"No. But you can have them if you want."

"Never. But really — what *are* you going to do with them?"

"I won't let the Commodore or Hakim get them. They've got enough. Maybe I'll go shark fishing myself — tomorrow or next week — and find them. Maybe I'll turn them over to the Foundation for the Junior Blind. I'm not sure yet. You know, Angel — you look a little more Chinese tonight — like Gene Tierney did in *The Shanghai Gesture.* She was a half-caste named Poppy. Ona Munson played Mother Gin Sling. There was this scene where Poppy came to —"

"Sam."

"Yeah?"

She lifted the sheet that covered her and was naked before him.

"Shut up, Sam, and come to bed."

He lifted the glass of brandy toward his lips. "Yeah — here's looking at you, kid."

For a while the Eyes of Alexander laughed and danced on the white sheet. Then they fell to the floor.

We hope you have enjoyed this Large Print book. Other Thorndike Press or Chivers Press Large Print books are available at your library or directly from the publishers.

For more information about current and upcoming titles, please call or write, without obligation, to:

Thorndike Press
295 Kennedy Memorial Drive
Waterville, ME 04901
Tel. (800) 223-1244

OR

Chivers Press Limited
Windsor Bridge Road
Bath BA2 3AX
England
Tel. (0225) 335336

All our Large Print titles are designed for easy reading, and all our books are made to last.